12.95

TROUBLE
IN
PARADISE

TROUBLE IN PARADISE

by

Pierre Boulle

TRANSLATED FROM THE FRENCH BY
Patricia Wolf

THE VANGUARD PRESS
NEW YORK

Library of Congress Cataloging in Publication Data

Boulle, Pierre, 1912–
    Trouble in paradise.

    Translation of: Les coulisses du ciel.
    I. Title.
PQ2603.0754C6513   1985   843'.914   85-650
ISBN 0-8149-0897-7

Designer: Tom Bevans
Manufactured in the United States of America.

PART ONE

THREE
SEPARATE
PERSONS

I

The Society for New Psychical Research deserved the excellent reputation it had earned throughout Europe. Only well-balanced individuals were permitted to apply, preferably those accustomed to rigorous methods of investigation. Thus it could rightfully claim to have escaped the taint of mysticism, not to mention the hysteria or downright quackery that had infected similar organizations in the past. Its members included several established scientists of a liberal bent who were willing to consider any new and even outlandish theory, but insisted on testing it repeatedly under closely controlled experimental conditions.

· · · 3 · · ·

One of these individuals was Marcole the astrophysicist. This noted theoretician had become convinced in the course of his own research and reflections that the spirit was not the exclusive endowment and privilege of human beings but existed throughout the universe. Being a skeptic, he would not reject a priori the possibility of communicating with that spirit through some appropriate medium. Marcole was among the six persons gathered that evening in the drawing room in Paris of Mme de Fonteneige, all hopeful of witnessing such a manifestation.

The hostess, Mme de Fonteneige, president of the Association for the Dignity of Women and active in several other organizations, instinctively gravitated toward elitist groups. Although she had no professional qualifications to speak of, she was a good observer, kept a cool head, and had been accepted on the strength of her social status.

The third person attending this evening's séance was no less than the chief of state, President Dumont-Gayol. He was not a member of the Society, but came to meetings now and then out of curiosity and to relax from the tiresome round of official duties. He and Mme de Fonteneige were old friends. Through her many influential contacts, she had helped him in the course of his political career, just as she had helped other politicians, artists, and writers by swinging votes in favor of their election to an assembly or a learned society.

Two churchmen bore witness to the group's serious and highly moral purpose. Father Routier had studied science in his younger days and had graduated from one of the top universities the same year as Marcole, with whom he was on a first-name basis. Later, after turning his back on the world, Routier took up religion. He became a pillar of the Catholic church, developed close ties to the Vatican, and would have become a bishop long before—with or without help from Mme de Fonteneige, who also had friends in high ecclesiastic places—if he had wanted to and if a modest title had not been more in keeping with his religious duties. His mission was to cruise in social circles, study them firsthand, and come up with a program for spreading the faith. He refused to believe in roving spirits and had joined the Society for New Psychical Research purely out of duty and curiosity.

Being an ecumenical activist, Routier kept in touch regularly with a number of Protestant ministers working for the same goals and had been instrumental in recruiting the Reverend Mr. Roberts, who was also present that evening, to the Society. This Scotsman, a scholar who could quote from the Encyclopedia Britannica as readily as the Bible, also specialized in Oriental languages. The prospect of evoking phantoms had struck him as altogether irresistible.

The sixth guest was a timid, self-effacing young woman whose name Mme de Fonteneige and the others had long since forgotten. They simply referred to her by the job she performed: the medium. Medium she was indeed, having proved beyond a doubt her extrasensory talents in previous sessions. Through her agency, and barring any possibility of a hoax, several experiments had been carried out that compelled objective minds to do some serious thinking: telepathy, clairvoyance, automatic writing, phrases in a language she didn't know, and even different apparitions of hands and human faces. Marcole surmised that interference between mind and matter might account for these manifestations. Father Routier, who often discussed the subject with him, could hardly deny the physical nature of the occurrences in view of the care taken to avoid mystification. "I consider them mental impressions," he said, "perhaps caused by telepathic phenomena that I'm forced to recognize, although they're not objective realities."

The astrophysicist shook his head thoughtfully and concluded with the cautious observation that he would have to reserve judgment until many more experiments had been performed. With the help of a medium, however, he had little doubt that someday they would witness some genuinely revealing phenomena.

That was more or less the opinion and the hope of Reverend Roberts, who took issue on the following point with Father Routier. "If we assume dead persons continue to exist—and I think we all believe that— then there's nothing irrational or irreverent about admitting they are able to communicate certain information to us."

"That's not in the Bible," protested Routier.

"No, but it's in the Encyclopedia Britannica," the Scottish minister snorted triumphantly.

o   o   o

It was not through the medium but through Marcole himself on that very evening that the first manifestation took place suggesting some supernatural presence.

"I'm here," he announced suddenly.

The others stared at him in disbelief. It was indeed the astrophysicist's voice, but with a peculiar inflection that was hard to place. It seemed to come from far away, yet sounded perfectly distinct. As usual, the members of the séance had joined hands and were sitting around a table waiting silently for a signal from the spirit world.

"I'm here," repeated the oddly unfamiliar voice of Marcole, this time with a trace of impatience.

"Who is it?" Reverend Roberts asked with sudden interest.

"The Spirit. I'm answering the question someone asked."

"I protest," exclaimed Father Routier. "Nobody asked the question, 'Spirit, are you there?' This sort of infantile behavior runs contrary to our rules of order."

"I did ask it mentally," Mme de Fonteneige confessed. "It's something I'm forever doing. I can't help it."

"I've done the same thing," President Dumont-Gayol admitted. "Please excuse me, father. I thought it was just part of the séance."

"And I repeat my answer: I'm here. The Spirit is here."

"Marcole, I wouldn't have believed you capable of such childishness," Father Routier protested. With an indignant shrug, he broke the chain of hands and was about to stand up.

The voice continued. "It would be a mistake for you to leave us, father—I think that's what they call you down here—because we're going to need some religious instruction. I'm the first to admit it. Besides, don't think that your leaving will stop me from inhabiting your friend M. Marcole's body, where I feel very much at home, or from speaking through his voice."

The tone had become so imperious that Father Routier hesitated and sat down again.

President Dumont-Gayol ventured to ask, "Who are you?"

"I'm getting tired of telling you over and over again: the Spirit."

"Whose spirit?"

"No human being's," the voice replied with a tinge of condescending irony. "Not a spirit but *the* Spirit, with a capital S, if you like. I'm talking to you in particular, father, and you also, reverend, because you both invoke me often in your prayers and should recognize me easily. Must I spell it out? I'm the one you call the Holy Spirit or the Third Person."

"That's the limit!" Father Routier exploded. "Marcole, will you kindly end this idiotic joke before it descends to blasphemy."

The astrophysicist replied in his normal voice, "It's not my doing, Routier. You have my word for it. I have to believe this because whoever spoke to you a moment ago through my lips was not I."

"Your incredulity astonishes me, gentlemen," continued the odd-sounding and mildly derisive voice. "Didn't you come here this evening to communicate with the spiritual essence of the universe? And when the Spirit itself addresses you, Spirit pure and unadulterated, why, you treat it like an imposter!"

Marcole's normal voice took up the conversation. "He's right. But first, Holy Spirit, may I respectfully ask a question that's been puzzling me?"

"Go right ahead."

"Why do you manifest yourself through me when you have a perfectly good medium available for such demonstrations?"

"Yes, why?" Father Routier chimed in, his suspicions mounting, for this dialogue between one and the same person was beginning to get on his nerves.

"Father," the Holy Ghost began very softly, "do you doubt that the Spirit breathes where it chooses?"

"That's not what I meant to say, but..."

"And if it breathes where it chooses, why shouldn't it choose to appear to those most worthy to receive it?"

"Thank you," the astrophysicist interrupted.

· · · 9 · · ·

"Don't mention it. The warmest reception doesn't necessarily indicate intelligence. I've been wrong on occasion and have even ended up among hopeless imbeciles after thinking I had sensed an affinity between them and myself. It was an illusion. They would have welcomed any kind of nonsense and lacked genuine curiosity. I must add, M. Marcole, that you don't fall into that category."

"Thanks again."

"I tried first to enter you, father," the Holy Spirit continued, addressing Routier, "but the resistance was too great and I gave up."

"My pleasure," muttered the priest.

"I'm sure I would have succeeded if I'd kept at it, but I was drawn to M. Marcole. As for that woman you call a psychic, I felt no attraction to her. Still, I think she can probably help us perform another experiment."

"What about me?" "And me?" came a duet from the head of state and Mme de Fonteneige, who seemed vexed at having been left out of the conversation.

The Spirit smiled through Marcole's countenance and paused a moment to formulate an evasive reply. "I felt you were a bit too involved in superficial thoughts for the moment."

Mme de Fonteneige and the president fell into a brooding silence.

Reverend Roberts seemed impressed and took up the conversation. "I might be inclined to believe you ... but tell me first, what am I to call you?"

"You may call me Lord, for I'm supposed to be the Divine Spirit. Isn't that one of your teachings? I'm the Third Person. Only I don't think you should rely on me to supply the proper labels."

"Well now, Lord, please forgive us," Roberts responded, "we're only poor mortals forever expecting to be led astray by deceptive appearances. We've been duped so often that we now require visible scientific proof if we're to be convinced. Forgive me again, Lord, but couldn't you produce some concrete evidence?"

"Now, there's a reasonable request," said the Spirit. "I must admit that I quite accept the fact that no one grants me blind credulity, and I rather enjoy the lengthy process of persuading people who hold reasonable doubts. My dear reverend, I anticipated your request and plan to present you very shortly with evidence as visible and tangible as the most hardened skeptics among you could desire. As I'm pure spirit, having never possessed a body, you'll understand that I can't appear to you. But I've brought someone with me from heaven, a majestic personality, who *can* appear and is quite prepared to do so."

At these words the pastor and the priest exchanged worried glances. "What kind of mischief are we in for now?" protested Routier. "Marcole, for the last time, I beg you to end this tasteless joke."

The Spirit ignored the interruption and continued. "If the medium, whose talents we all recognize, would be good enough to will this manifestation before she puts herself to sleep, you will see before you,

· · · 11 · · ·

incorruptible in all her glory, the witness I promised you, whom nobody is likely to challenge. May I ask your cooperation by remaining silent and calm."

Instinctively, they all obeyed the voice, whose authoritative delivery now seemed to defy resistance. With arms folded over her breast, the medium dozed off gradually as her features relaxed. Father Routier prayed for forgiveness for taking part in a ceremony that smelled faintly of heresy.

The awaited miracle arrived. No sooner had the psychic fallen asleep than a diaphanous cloud appeared to drift out of her body, solid haze at first, but gradually condensing and sharpening into an outline as the apparition began to fill out in the darkened room, which the emerging form seemed to illuminate. When the materialization was complete, witnesses to this marvel found themselves staring at a woman in her fifties wearing a long, loose-fitting gown of no identifiable color, her hair held in place by a veil framing the perfect oval of her gentle, mournful face—a face full of goodness and of anxiety, too, as if the memory of ancient events had etched an indelible sadness on her features.

"Jesus and Mary!" exclaimed Father Routier. Despite his excitement, he felt a peculiar rush of relief. Glancing furtively at the pastor, he detected the same reaction. For just a moment after the Spirit's announcement, both of them had experienced a subconscious dread that a personality even more awesome than this might appear. Everyone else remained tongue-tied with amazement.

Now entirely free of the medium, the woman gave a smile—of reassurance, it seemed—and said a few words that nobody understood save Reverend Roberts, the expert on Oriental languages. He trembled and listened intently.

When the woman had finished speaking, the Holy Spirit addressed him. "I suspect this is no mystery to you, reverend."

"No, indeed," the pastor spluttered. "I couldn't catch every single word because the accent is quite different from what I learned in school. But there can be no doubt, gentlemen: this is Aramaic."

"Aramaic!" exclaimed Father Routier. "The language spoken by Christ!"

"And, of course, by his mother," added the Spirit. "Could you translate for us what you just heard, reverend, or shall I?"

"I'll do it," Roberts declared in a voice quivering with emotion. "I may have missed a word or two, but in substance, this . . . this lady said, 'I am Mary, mother of Christ, mother of God. Don't be afraid. I have descended to earth not to harm anyone but, as the Holy Spirit, my companion, will confirm, to see what the two of us can do to improve the troubled situation we now have in heaven, which is upsetting everyone, myself most of all.'"

II

"I'm dreaming. These things are impossible," Father Routier stammered, mopping his brow.

"I don't understand your astonishment, father," said the Holy Ghost. "Just as I'm in the best position to respond to those in search of spiritual manifestations, it stands to reason that the person best qualified (along with Jesus Christ, who's a special case) to return to earth, having once left it, is none other than the Holy Virgin. For Mary never knew the bondage of mortality and decay since she rose directly to heaven, body and soul, her assumption ordained centuries ago

• • • 14 • • •

by Christians, the doctrine of which was declared by your Pope Pius XII. I doubt that you wish to take issue with a papal edict."

"I like this argument," Marcole interjected.

"This argument..." Father Routier began and stopped short, suddenly terrified that he might be about to utter a heresy.

"The Reformation never asserted that," murmured the minister. "Yet there she is, right in front of us."

"Yes, it's true, there she is," the bewildered priest mumbled.

"There she is!" crowed Mme de Fonteneige. "There she is! The Queen of Heaven, the Madonna, the Holy Mother of God! She has chosen to appear in *my* drawing room! What an honor!"

"She has chosen France!" President Dumont-Gayol declared proudly in a burst of patriotic zeal. "This can't be a mere stroke of fortune."

Father Routier no longer was in any condition to make a rational objection and took refuge in prayer. The Holy Ghost waited for the members to regain their composure before continuing. "You see her now and will go on seeing her for some time to come because she intends to sojourn among you. She is now entirely free of the medium, who is about to wake up. You may also turn on all the lights, which won't scare Mary, and I personally am put off by this semidarkness you seem so fond of."

Mme de Fonteneige rose and went to press a number of buttons, then returned to her seat. Mary, who still stood facing her stupefied audience with a gentle smile on her lips, reflected the light from the chandelier and the table lamps in a way that struck the hostess as decidedly supernatural.

"Now you can see her better," said the Spirit. "If anyone is still in doubt, you may touch her robe, her hands, her face, and convince yourself it is indeed she in the flesh, she whose glorious body departed this earth nearly two thousand years ago, perfectly intact as your church fathers decreed—after endless squabbles and beatings about the bush, I might add. It is she herself, not a phantom as I feel Reverend Roberts is inclined to believe, nor a mental projection as you sometimes tend to explain such phenomena, father."

Encouraged by the Spirit, Marcole was the first to approach Mary, whose smile reassured him. He clasped her hands, then slowly ran his fingers over her face and, with a respectful bow, returned to his chair, nodding his head in approval. President Dumont-Gayol stepped up next. Having resisted the gallant impulse to plant a kiss on the outstretched fingertips, he wavered, uncertain how to handle himself at such a high-level meeting, then finally patted Mary's shoulder protectively and returned to his seat in silence. Father Routier made a gesture of fierce denial and tried to go on praying. Reverend Roberts took three steps forward, dropped to his knees, and, grasping the hem of Mary's gown with trembling fingers, kissed it fervently. As for Mme de Fonteneige— the least intimidated and the most excited—she cried out, "Dear heart! I mean dear Holy Mother! Let me clasp you in my arms!"

Mary acquiesced, beaming now, and as the hostess hugged her wildly, the celestial Virgin acknowledged these effusions with dignified restraint.

When everyone was seated again, the Holy Spirit continued speaking through Marcole's lips. "I can appreciate your excitement," he began. "Still, it shouldn't make you overlook the most elementary rules of hospitality, which must be the same on earth as in heaven. I should think you could offer your Blessed Mother a chair for lack of the glorious throne she deserves, as we have a great deal to tell you this evening and it would hardly be fitting for the Queen of Heaven to stand on her feet among six comfortably seated earthlings."

At this reproach the president turned scarlet, leaped out of his chair and offered it to Mary. She thanked him with a nod as she sat down and said something in Aramaic, translated by Reverend Roberts with occasional interruptions from the Spirit to correct a word here and there.

"I've spent more time kneeling than sitting," she observed, "and not just during my earthly existence, as you must be aware, for in the last centuries of my sojourn in heaven I've endured much distress and disappointment, as the Holy Ghost will undoubtedly tell you. Alas, for some time now I've been at a loss to know where to direct my prayers or even to whom."

"I've been plagued by the same worries and still am," declared the Spirit. "This also applies to the angels and the chosen ones who attend us in the celestial spheres."

There was a moment of leaden silence as everyone heard the gravity of these declarations; each was dying of curiosity, yet didn't dare ask questions.

The Spirit went on rather solemnly. "My dear friends—let me call you friends, for it would be tedious to address all of you by your proper names— we owe you an explanation for breaking into your meeting. I'll tell you briefly why we have appeared on earth. The misfortune that has been infecting the climate of heaven for ages is this: the Father and Son don't get along anymore."

The two clerics burst into an indignant chorus and were preparing to follow this up with a violent protest, but the Holy Spirit would brook no interruption. "The Father and Son can't get along anymore! Don't you see what this discord implies? They quarrel over everything and nothing, the critical issues as well as the trifles. The Father mistrusts the Son and is jealous of him. The Son contests the Father's decisions and openly defies him. This strife has worsened over the centuries, to the point where the angels are dazed and the saints at wit's end."

He paused again, seemingly overwhelmed by the mere articulation of the problem, while his audience gazed wide-eyed with wonder. Having composed himself, he pursued his tale. "If you like, I'll tell you how this sad situation came about. Then you'll understand how desperate we feel and why Mary and I came to earth to try to think things out and perhaps seek a helping hand, or at least a helpful hint, that we'll never get in heaven."

Here is the story told by the Holy Spirit through the lips of Marcole the astrophysicist, with comments added by Mary, who insisted on elaborating certain points.

III

After his resurrection and ascension, Christ was greeted at the gates of heaven by choirs of saints and angels singing his praises. All martyrs in his behalf were given a similar reception. Not a single sour note marred the festivities. The Father embraced his son and called him "beloved" while the celestial hosts echoed the word with shouts of acclamation. The Father awarded him a place in his court of honor and throughout this period of rejoicing lavished on him the marks of esteem he felt had been earned by a creature who had venerated and served him faithfully.

A creature! The trouble started when that term was challenged, first on earth and then with such fierce passion that the echoes rose to the heavens and sowed dissension like the plague. The Father's brow darkened when he observed the frenzied devotion of the early Christians under the influence of Christ's disciples. Theologians soon fell into step behind humble worshipers, while the Father stood by helplessly, with growing hostility, and watched the superhuman efforts they were making to meet the demands of an expanding community that clamored for deification of the Son. The emergence of this new religion, based on the doctrine of the Trinity, loomed in the Father's eye as a menace and a flagrant insult.

Having to divide up his godship among three separate persons was humiliating enough, but far more painful was the realization that Christ's image tended to overwhelm his own, first on earth and soon, by osmosis, in heaven, and was gradually claiming the homage he wanted for himself. Paul, a remarkable visionary, had engineered that. Yet, soon after the apostle to the Gentiles had met a martyr's death, hadn't he, the Father, grudgingly consented to admit him to heaven, knowing that if he didn't, it would irritate portions of the celestial community? For Paul's eloquence had won him widespread sympathy in paradise, especially among angels of the ninth order, who were in the majority.

o   o   o

The Holy Spirit had reeled off this scenario while Mary continued to look thoughtful and resigned. During a pause, the astrophysicist Marcole regained his own personality and asked the very question that was in everyone's mind. "Lord, we're all stunned. I do believe in you, and since I feel your presence within me, who should know better than I that what you say is true. But you must forgive our dismay. On this planet we had heard thus far about the revolt of the wicked angels, but we had no inkling the revolt centered on the Son and not Satan. Even the boldest among us could scarcely imagine a rivalry springing up between the Father and the Son."

"The rivalry arose in the early centuries of this era," declared the Spirit, "and has simply intensified. Furthermore, as you know, the rebellion of the wicked angels was quelled in no time by the Father when he hurled its leader, Satan, into the darkness, but the revolt of the Son and his followers proved far more distressing because he couldn't send his legions of warrior archangels against them."

"Why not?" Mme de Fonteneige asked innocently.

"Imagine the effect it would have had on the Catholic church! Many archangels would have refused to take arms against an individual then widely coming to be regarded as the divine essence in accordance with Paul's teachings. I suspect, too, that the Father felt pressured by your doctrine of the Trinity and feared that the battle might develop into a struggle against him and even turn his ultimate victory into a tragic defeat. Now, have you any other questions or shall I continue?"

"Please go on, Lord," Marcole urged. "I have a list of questions to ask, but finish your story first."

o   o   o

Thus a restless uncertainty clouded the heavens. At any rate, after the first skirmishes it occurred to the Holy Ghost that a kind of *modus vivendi* might be arrived at if the Father would refrain from openly publicizing the Son's prerogatives and the Son would refrain from defying the Father. In fact, both felt unsure of themselves: the doctrine of the Trinity had come between them and sown dissension. Being on good terms with both, the Holy Ghost learned this from their confidential complaints, and since his personality was not clearly defined as yet, he was able to play a conciliatory role, which he did. It was he who advised the Father to award the place of honor at his right hand to the Son instead of a back bench at court. The Father made this concession as a gesture of appeasement.

But celestial eyes focused on the earth, where turmoil reigned as a reflection of the problems in heaven that were constantly debated by passionate orators in tumultuous assemblies. After several centuries of this war of words, which came to blows now and then, the Father grew interested in the personality of Arius and spent more time studying Arianism than any other creed. And when Arius, disciple of Lucian, declared that whatever merits or superiority Jesus Christ had over other creatures, he remained a creation of the Father, the latter agreed heartily. Ever since he had started to brood over this question, the Father had resigned himself to the prospect of having to relax his demands somewhat, to make new concessions, and to admit the Son's close relationship: a kind of demigod—provided that he, the Father, continue to be recognized as the sole creator of all living things. The thesis put forth by Arius appeared to be an acceptable compromise. The Holy Spirit used all his persuasive powers to convince the Father that this position was both reasonable and likely to win popular approval.

It came as a surprise to him, and a rude shock to the Father, when they heard that Alexander of Alexandria, after flirting with Arianism, had turned against his priest Arius and banished him. The shock was even greater when, in 325, at the Council of Nicea, the church fathers declared Arianism a heresy, solemnly proclaimed the Son to be consubstantial and eternal with the Father, and denounced any notion of his creation by or subordination to the Father as sacrilege.

The Holy Spirit never was one to hold grudges.

He greeted this decree with a sigh and puzzled over the logic of it, for he was a great believer in universal reason. But the Almighty threw a fit violent enough to make the heavens tremble. His hopes revived and he calmed down somewhat when it appeared that the incredible Nicene formulary was not generally accepted, that the religious authorities were still debating the issue in stormy synods, and that Constantine, under the sway of two influential leaders, Eusebius of Caesarea and Eusebius of Nicomedia, seemed prepared to re-examine Arianism. A weary Constantine died prematurely, and a year later the archheretic followed him to the grave just when he might have been rehabilitated, so uncertain was opinion as to the real nature of the Son.

The Father threw open the gates of paradise to welcome the heresiarch and exhorted him to expound his doctrine in heaven since it hadn't met much success on earth. A few years later he went so far as to reconvene the Council of Nicea with most of the original cast, now defunct, in attendance. But all his efforts to win them over to his view met with scant success, and he felt that he had failed.

Torn by their fears of antagonizing the Father or neutralizing the Son, and bound by a previous decree that had been divinely inspired, the council came up with a nonpartisan formula that pleased nobody and left unsolved the central issue. This council was never heard of on earth, which led the Holy Spirit to remark that in matters of religion, celestial efforts had little impact on terrestrial decisions.

In the year 381 the Council of Constantinople ratified the Nicene formulary establishing the doctrine of the consubstantiality of Father and Son. The Christian world surrendered at last to this dogma, except for the Father and his loyal following.

IV

"After the last council," the Spirit concluded, "the strife between Father and Son got worse, to the point where there was no hope of reconciliation. . . . I think I've given you a pretty accurate picture of the crisis in paradise."

Impressed by the tale they had just heard, the members remained silent for a long time. The priest and the minister went on mumbling their prayers, crossing themselves frequently as if to ward off some evil charm. Mme de Fonteneige looked awed and exhilarated: this meeting was surpassing her wildest ambitions. President Dumont-Gayol appeared lost in thought, as if the evening's events had opened new worlds.

Once again Marcole took the initiative and asked a question in his normal voice. "Lord, you've shown us an attitude of the Father's we never suspected, but you've said practically nothing about the Son. How did he behave during this period? Was he respectful, at least outwardly? Or did he treat him as an equal and thus defy him?"

"This is something Mary can tell you," replied the Spirit, "for she has followed the Son's development more closely than anyone, and has suffered for it. I think she can express herself in French now, as I've no doubt she's learned the language just by listening to us."

"I can speak it indeed," Mary confirmed. And in her soft voice tinged with melancholy, punctuated with occasional bursts of passion, Mary began to recount her own observations from the time she first set foot in paradise.

o   o   o

When the Blessed Virgin reached heaven after her miraculous Assumption, the reception she met was dignified though unenthusiastic. A handful of angels and a sprinkling of the chosen greeted her as the mother of God, but clearly she was no star attraction. It never crossed her mind to feel offended by the modest appointment or lowly honors she received.

The Son was polite but distant, displaying the same slightly superior attitude he had shown her on earth. Actually, he paid scant attention to her at first, still behaving like a dutiful son to the Father and accepting his authority without a murmur, apparently satisfied with his station in the hierarchy. Mary was gratified by this harmony and resigned herself to feeling somewhat neglected.

The friendly understanding didn't last very long; the Son's attitude changed. The religious turmoil on earth began to perturb him, then to exhilarate him like a stiff dose of spirits. He couldn't ignore it— actually, he trembled with excitement at the hymns to his glory, at the passionate devotions tending to elevate him alongside the Father and thus to supplant the latter in certain religious quarters.

When the Arianistic crisis broke and the heretic from Alexandria began propagating the theme of the Son's dependency, Christ felt cruelly disappointed and humiliated to see the movement attract so many supporters.

o   o   o

"I remember," said Mary. "That was the time he made up with me. Instead of ignoring me, he seemed overly eager to please, at least on the surface. He treated me more respectfully and showed some degree of affection. That corresponded to the moment when people on earth began calling me the mother of God instead of the mother of Christ. I had no illusions about the motives behind this change. It was a pose and, as I soon found out, quite artificial, but it made me happy all the same. Sometimes he would confide his anxieties to me and we talked as mother and son, which never had happened before, either on earth or in heaven.

"He mentioned Arius one night, complaining bitterly that the wretched infidel wanted to make him a demigod, one of those creatures with whom pagans people the sky! 'Demigod! Demigod,' he kept saying wearily. 'Aren't you the mother of a full-fledged god?' From then on he insisted that I always be addressed as 'Mother of God'."

o   o   o

Like the Father, the Son was an avid follower of council debates, but with different expectations. When at last his eternal existence and divine essence were decreed, his behavior changed. Less than modest in his triumph, he appeared insolent and openly defiant of the Almighty. At that moment the two individuals began to quarrel about all the problems in heaven, each intent on imposing his own will as if to publicize how very different they were—which no one doubted to start with. The Father loved to display his iron discipline, to separate the good souls from the bad and chastise the latter mercilessly. Each time he laid down his law, the Son was there to preach just a little louder his message of love, based on forgiveness of sins ("Didn't I redeem them once and for all?" he would shout) and pardon of offenses, to the point of contending that the good and the not-so-good were equally entitled to divine favor, which made the Father furious.

o   o   o

"But this gentleness and mercy that he preached so tirelessly never humbled him," said Mary with a wry smile of disenchantment. "I became convinced it was a pose, which some of the Father's liegemen denounced as hypocrisy. Our relationship quickly deteriorated as a result of his boundless ambition. I've said that it brought us closer in the beginning, when he insisted that I be treated like a queen and commanded the saints and angels to kneel before me— something I never enjoyed because I felt he did it for his own satisfaction. But in time even this indirect homage seemed out of place to him. He had come to regard me as an instrument, a mere machine that the one and only God had created for the sole purpose of begetting him in the form of the Son.

"I knew he was deeply hurt by the proclamation of Nestorius that no longer was I to be called Theotokos, meaning mother of God, but simply Christotokos. What irked him most about the heretical preaching of this patriarch of Constantinople was not the diminution of my person, which meant nothing to him, but the implied assault on his own, which is all he cared about. 'Christotokos! Christotokos!' he complained to the four corners of paradise. Arianism was rearing its ugly head! 'My mother is Theotokos!'

"In the year 430, with feverish excitement, hour after hour, he followed the debates of the Synod of Rome. He was elated when Pope Celestine confirmed my title of Theotokos, then infuriated by the mild papal reprimand to Nestorius, who was merely admonished to renounce his error. He didn't simmer down for a whole year, until the Council of Ephesus prevailed on certain bishops to condemn the heresy and deny Nestorius Holy Communion, a decision that met with great popular support and a display of fireworks. That marked a great triumph for the Son. When it came to attacks on his own person, his doctrine of forgiveness became blurred."

"Holy Mother, forgive me for interrupting," Marcole broke in, "but I'm rather surprised that you and the Spirit examined so closely the goings on at all those councils during our era. You remember every detail and every date."

"It's an indisputable fact," the Holy Spirit confessed, "that what happens downstairs is of great interest upstairs."

Mary's unassuming countenance suddenly contracted into an angry scowl. "Your councils!" she blurted out. "Sometimes I wonder if they weren't the root of all our griefs, especially the ones my son is causing. It's hard for me to remember that for a time on earth he abhorred theologians, and now he prays frantically to them to cast a vote in his favor. As for me, Mary, I've endured far greater torments than anyone because of their rude and impertinent remarks about my person. I've been martyred in spirit as well as in the flesh. The church fathers heaped worse indignities on me than on any mortal creature on earth, in heaven, or in hell. Every inch of my body has been fingered and every organ displayed publicly, causing untold distress to my loyal followers, jubilation to the faithless, and utter humiliation to me."

"Pardon my interrupting again, Mother of God," Marcole broke in, "but you speak as if the councils had turned you into some unbelievably monstrous accident of nature whom you now reject. By letting yourself get so upset, aren't you simply confirming their conclusions? In your own words, what do you feel is your true essence?"

Mary fell silent for a long time, as if pondering the meaning of a complicated question. When she finally answered, her muffled voice betrayed a profound bewilderment. "In my heart and conscience, I'm not sure of anything." She brooded a while longer, then resumed in a livelier mood. "I'm uncertain, don't you see? When all this palaver started about my perpetual virginity, I thought it was indecent, even outrageous. It exasperated me and made me want to rebel. Then, as the debate continued, I began to have doubts. The Holy Spirit has told you how earthly decisions send their echo into the skies. Perhaps even farther— who knows? All of us up there have a kind of inferiority complex with regard to doctrines established down here. After all, I had only a confused recollection of Christ's conception, which could have been just a dream that faded in the hysteria of those clamorous ecumenical councils. When Pope Pius IX decreed that not only was I immaculate but innocent of sin as well— even the original sin—it became an article of faith. I felt obligated to hush my rebellious inner voice.

"Later, however, my uncertainty and doubts revived on the subject of my rise to heaven—my Assumption, as you call it—an event that raised havoc in the hearts of all believers and began to preoccupy the religious authorities, owing to public pressure, once they had settled the issue of my virginity."

"It's a fact," observed Reverend Roberts, "that the cult of Mary took root among the poor. In the century after the doctrine of the Immaculate Conception was declared, eight million petitions reached the Vatican asking for clarification of the circumstances surrounding her glorious Assumption."

"Eight million!" exclaimed President Dumont-Gayol, whose head was filled with statistics related to a recent poll. "Nobody can resist such pressure."

"Pius XII didn't resist," said Mary. "On November 1, 1950, according to your dating system (it was only yesterday, you see, which is why I still feel nervous about it), he declared ex cathedra that I had ascended to heaven, body and soul, in the same manner as had the Son. That also became the official creed and I guess I had no choice but to accept it."

She was calmer now and her modest demeanor had returned along with her smile. "All things considered, this doctrine must contain a grain of truth, since here I am, returned among you, body and soul."

V

The astrophysicist Marcole, whose features relaxed perceptibly as soon as the Spirit ceased to possess him, asked another question, proving that his periodic withdrawals did not prevent him from following and maintaining a lively interest in the conversation. "But you, Lord, you who borrow my person in order to manifest yourself—which I consider an honor—you must feel as concerned as the Son about the mystery of the Trinity. Are you convinced you're both the Third Person and Eternal God? If so, hasn't some hostility impaired your relations with the Father or the Son, with the same deplorable results you've just described between those two? If I'm not mistaken, the church fathers have argued as persistently and ferociously over your divine nature as over the others and decreed your godhood only after endless controversy."

"Friend," replied the Spirit, "your question reveals the admirable probing mind of a passionate seeker after truth who is not put off by fear of blasphemy. The same can't be said at the moment for either Father Routier or Reverend Roberts, who are wondering if they're not committing some awful sin by listening to statements that may be inspired by the devil. To satisfy your curiosity, friend, let me tell you that I've been assigned so many different personalities since the beginning of time that I decided to remain undecided, and this state of mind doesn't bother me at all. I have no ambitions. I recognize that while some equate me with God, others don't, and I'm not the least offended. In fact, the idea of quibbling over the question strikes me as frivolous. Perhaps this facet of my nature comes from never having had a body."

"You really never had a body? That's the hardest thing for me to understand, being a materialist who believes the spirit is everywhere. To me, however, 'everywhere' means wherever there is matter."

"I've had occasion to regret it, but that's the way it is. You can be the judge. I've assumed all kinds of appearances. In the early ages of your awakened consciousness, I was the wind, imagined as a kind of pagan divinity. Later, when the Israelites conceived of Yahweh as the omnipotent deity, I became more or less the expression of his vital force. After that, among certain sects I was associated with man: I was his breath, identified with his soul. Next, I acted as a kind of link between man and God, an incarnation that was particularly enjoyable, I must admit. Only with the advent of Christianity did I become the Third Person of the Holy Trinity.

"Alas, even that person underwent further metamorphosis. Certain theologians (whose competence couldn't be discounted) wanted to subordinate me to the Son, just as the disciples of Arius subordinated the Son to the Father. Others denied me the designation of Holy Spirit and lumped me instead with a multitude of celestial spirits not unlike the angels. Still others doubted my existence as an individual entity, and at one time I rather agreed with that view. I wasn't offended by being labeled a mere emanation. This last suggestion, which is found in Hermas and in Tatian, seemed natural and sensible enough, but the authors of it were denigrated and once again your councils decreed otherwise. An article of faith establishes me as a god apart as well as an individual personality. I don't understand it, but, like Mary, I accept it—and await future developments.

"Briefly then, most of the principals in heaven have allowed themselves to be influenced by your theologians, but with varying emotions: the Son, with pride born of their decisions; Mary, with resignation inspired by a slight case of doubt; and myself, with indifference. Only the Father fiercely contests the imposition of such highhanded authority. He won't rest until these dogmas are rescinded, and his bad temper makes life in heaven intolerable. Now you know just about everything that goes on upstairs."

"Intolerable? Really?" Dumont-Gayol asked. "I suppose that's why you left?"

"Not exactly," replied the Spirit. "Our own well-being isn't all that motivates us. Mary and I have a higher purpose. The reason you find us here tonight, the reason we plan to make an extended visit on earth, is in the hope of restoring peace and harmony to heaven."

"A noble purpose," observed the president. "May I ask, Lord, how you plan to carry out this program?"

"You must understand, sir, that Mary and I have great respect for the Father's judgment. His intransigence and obstinacy make us suspect that some errors may have crept into the council decisions."

"What then?"

"Well, the picture created by the church fathers can be retouched by other church fathers. What councils and popes have decreed, future councils and popes can modify. That's the task before me, and Mary has said she is ready to help. With just a few successive changes of dogma—each of which, of course, should make the public think that only minor details are affected—it should be possible to evolve definitions that satisfy the Father and amplify his image. I discussed this with Arius at some length before coming here and I think a solution should be sought in the doctrine he promoted. If we could work this out, I feel certain the Father would be willing to relent a bit, to stop being harsh almost to the point of cruelty, and listen once in a while when the Son preaches charity."

"But from what you've told us, Lord, about the Son's personality," Marcole pursued, "it's doubtful he would accept such a compromise."

"He's likely to rebel at the outset, but we hope he would yield in the end, if the earth's theologians remain firm and precise—and if the angels and saints, who have had enough of this anarchy, exert sufficient pressure. I speak of a group of wise men, depressed and silent until now, who might just raise their voices and shift the scales."

"The silent majority," observed Dumont-Gayol.

"Majority, I doubt, but a significant group all the same. As for me, since I don't pay much attention to matters of precedence, I'd be glad to accept a modest station—say, 'first deputy of the Son,' which would flatter his ego."

"That's a novel concept of the Trinity," declared Mme de Fonteneige.

"Maybe we ought to go a step further and give that mystery a thorough review," the Spirit murmured dreamily. "Oh, I've no illusions and I know it won't be easy. Most of your theologians are pigheaded. They cling to the judgments of their predecessors and don't even care to discuss them. 'Sacred tradition,' they call it. Still, I've overheard a number of conversations that suggest there's hope. After all, over the last fifty years I've watched some of them develop to the point where they can embrace a more humane concept of evolution and gradually accept an interpretation of the creation that differs considerably from sacred writ. The main thing is not to confront these gentlemen head on."

"To be more explicit, Lord," said the president, "how will you get the theologians to change their views?"

"As you can see, I'm able to inhabit human bodies, to replace their souls and guide them in the direction I choose. Often I encounter resistance, rarely a stone wall. I like to hope that the ecclesiastical authorities who debate and determine dogma are susceptible to the breath of the Holy Spirit. . . . Just as in your case, father," he went on, addressing Routier. "Though I experienced some difficulty using your person, I'm sure I would have succeeded in the long run, either by perseverance or by taking you unawares and having your lips deliver the statements I made through M. Marcole."

"Don't you dare!" the priest protested indignantly and with sudden confidence. "If it isn't you, Marcole, indulging in a horrid joke, then I know whose voice it is. You're unmasked, Satan, and I have a weapon that you can't resist. *Vade retro!*"

Staring straight into the astrophysicist's eyes, Routier made a solemn, sweeping sign of the cross. No sooner had he done this than his expression altered imperceptibly, and a strange note crept into his voice as he went on speaking. The other members of the group grasped the situation instantly.

"That sign, father," said the Holy Ghost through Routier's lips, "instead of repulsing me, attracts me like a magnet. You should have figured that out. Can you hear me and are you finally convinced I'm not the Evil One?"

"I hear you," the priest mumbled, regaining his normal voice. "I have to believe you're some supernatural creature. Lord, if you're really the Spirit, you must forgive me. I no longer know what to think."

"Calm yourself, dear father, I don't want to upset you anymore and I yield now to your desperate efforts to repel me. It's up to you to prove to Reverend Roberts that he is wrong to think this simple operation wouldn't work with him."

And indeed it was through the pastor's lips that the Spirit continued speaking. "My dear reverend, I urge you to stop plotting how to toss an inkwell in my face as your Martin Luther did to ward off the devil. You'd only hurt yourself because I'm within you. You must sense that I'm not Satan."

• • • 42 • • •

"I'll admit anything you wish, Lord," said Roberts, whose face had turned beet red, "but I beg you to leave me alone."

"That's just what I'm doing and will return for a while to the person of Marcole the scientist, who is far more accommodating than you. . . . Friends," he went on speaking through the astrophysicist's mouth, "don't think I've tried to impress you with my modest talents. I merely wanted to show you the evidence you asked for."

"Couldn't you . . . now couldn't you, Lord, harumpf. . ." the president interjected, coughing to clear his throat, "couldn't you possess me and inspire me too? There are times when I feel the need of it."

"We might arrange that, sir, and I promise to do it one day when you feel the need of it. But I'm not here tonight to play games. Mary and I have preparations to make, mostly in the way of information-gathering, which the Father has assigned us. We'll each use the method that suits us best."

"I have no power to substitute for a human soul," said Mary, "so my influence will be limited. But, unlike the Holy Spirit, I have a body and so can mingle with all sorts of creatures, converse with them, find out what believers are thinking and hoping . . . nonbelievers, too. I feel that public opinion in general ought to teach us a great deal."

"Don't worry, holy and humblehearted mother. The climate of opinion among the masses has always been the primary concern of decision-makers. Though I hope to influence some of the latter, I can never expect to turn them in a direction that runs counter to popular belief."

"I'll have to leave you now," Mary said as she got up from her chair. "I wouldn't want to abuse your hospitality any longer. I need to find lodgings, as well as some clothes more appropriate to this world than what I have on. Besides, I'll have to find work, a job that will bring me in contact with different levels of society. To do all that I need an assistant..."

"Look no further, Blessed Mary," Mme de Fonteneige exclaimed impulsively. "This is your home. You can do your work from here. Does it suit you?"

"Indeed it does, but I wouldn't want to impose on you."

"I beg you to accept, please, Holy Mother. What an honor! I'll stand in the shadow of your glory and let it reflect on me and give meaning to my every act. Consider this your home. We'll share everything like two sisters. Sisters!—what am I saying? I'm your very humble and devoted servant. An assistant, you said? There's nothing I wouldn't do to serve you."

"I'm most grateful," Mary replied.

"And if you should need a second assistant..." President Dumont-Gayol began. He had been thinking intently and frowning. "If you need support, it will be my pleasure to place the resources of the presidency at your disposal. We can discuss this later, Holy Mother, should the idea appeal to you."

Mary gave him a dignified nod of thanks.

In a voice so low that only Marcole heard it, the Holy Spirit murmured, "I was sure we'd encounter all this good will. My hunch was right to choose this house for our first appearance."

"As to presenting you to society," Mme de Fonteneige continued exuberantly, "you knocked at the right door. Holy Mother, I'll present you to the people who count in our country, and to every major political, literary, artistic, business, and religious association, including, of course, the Association for the Dignity of Women, of which I'm president. The ladies will be in seventh heaven, yes, literally among the angels, when they hear they are to meet you."

Mme de Fonteneige repeated "among the angels" several times, pronouncing each syllable with a beatific smile. Never before had she felt so euphoric. Having helped to elect one or two senators and academicians, and to secure the nomination of several bishops, now she could look forward to the climax of her social career: presenting the queen of heaven to society.

"Thank you again," said Mary, "but in the beginning, at least, I must remain incognito. For people to respond sincerely, it's best they not know my true identity."

· · · 45 · · ·

"And here am I with insider information!" declared Mme de Fonteneige ecstatically. "That's enough for me. . . . Tomorrow we'll visit my dressmaker. Meanwhile I'll let you try on some of my dresses this evening. We're the same size—what miraculous good fortune!" From the way she was hugging her waist with both hands as she noted the Virgin's measurements, it was apparent that she regarded the similarities not as a stroke of good fortune but as heaven's gift to her.

"Dear lady," said the Holy Ghost, "let me thank you in turn for your hospitality. It sets my mind at ease to know that Mary is in good hands. I have to go now," he added, as the astrophysicist rose to say goodby. "If you don't mind, my dear Marcole, I'll continue to inhabit you for a while—oh, don't worry, it'll be on and off, you know, and won't detract one bit from your character, which I suspect is very forceful. I can't think of any better lodging at the moment, and I feel I can learn a good deal through you."

"Be my guest, Lord," Marcole replied. "May our mutual association thrive."

As he bowed to the hostess, the Spirit added, "Friends, this is really not good-by, for I have a feeling we'll be talking again."

Mme de Fonteneige saw Marcole to the door, directing by turns a stream of polite small talk at the astrophysicist and a flurry of emotional protestations of devotion and gratitude at the Third Person. Each responded graciously to the slightly muddled phrases. As she turned back toward the drawing room, she felt overcome in the hallway by a surge of doubt that none of this had really happened and she would go back to find only the guests she had invited for the evening. It was with a great sense of relief that she saw all of them just where she had left them, gazing in disbelief at the smiling Madonna, who was still standing in the center of the room. Nobody had dared utter a word since the Spirit's departure.

Inspired by a sudden thought, Mme de Fonteneige broke the silence. "What a fool I am! The poor soul is probably worn out after such a journey. . . . Excuse me, dear Holy Mother," she apologized, "I'm unforgivable. I'll show you to your room. . . . Would you like a bath?"

"I don't think that will be necessary," said the Virgin, smiling. "Don't forget that I'm immaculate. My flesh and soul are immune to stain or blemish."

The two churchmen leaped to their feet and headed for the door, after first taking leave of the hostess and bowing low before Mary, with a quick genuflection added out of habit, which unconscious gesture Father Routier instantly regretted, shaking his head angrily. The young woman who had acted as medium followed them out.

"May I stay a while longer?" President Dumont-

Gayol asked the hostess as he continued to gaze thoughtfully at Mary. "I'd like to talk to you about something on my mind . . . I had an idea."

Mary drew aside discreetly and he continued. "Don't you think she's great? Appealing features, a sensitive, attractive face, and something more that I can't quite put my finger on."

"Yes, indeed. When I find her a hairdo to frame and enhance that pure oval face, I'm sure she'll make an impression that nobody who's anybody will forget."

"That's exactly what I was thinking," murmured the president. "Look after her and come back soon."

VI

Dumont-Gayol was still lost in thought when Mme de Fonteneige returned to the drawing room. Before saying a word, she collapsed wearily into an armchair, drained by the emotional experience behind her. "I put her in my own room. She insisted that I leave her alone and said she didn't need a thing except some rest," the hostess finally announced. "Please tell me that I'm not dreaming and this adventure really did happen. I couldn't bear to have my hopes dashed."

"My dear, I have asked myself the same question several times this evening. The answer is obvious.

These . . . creatures have given overwhelming proof of their supernatural character. It's all real. I'm trying to think how we can make the most of this extraordinary event."

"So am I, if I can manage to collect my wits," murmured Mme de Fonteneige. "I can already see her taking over the Association for the Dignity of Women. No one deserves the presidency more than she. I'll gladly step down if she accepts, but I can't see her in any lesser position."

"Certainly not, with her pedigree and appearance," replied Dumont-Gayol. "But I had in mind another equally honorable position for her. As a matter of fact, the two are not incompatible."

"What position?"

The head of state did not answer the question directly. "Have you noticed," he began in a voice tingling with excitement, "her extraordinary gift of assimilation? After listening to us for just a few minutes, she was able to pick up our language and speak it as well as you and I."

"Extraordinary indeed. Supernatural, I might say, which shouldn't astound us."

"This talent," the president went on, "should give her a definite edge in sensitive situations where others generally fail."

"Unquestionably."

"Besides that ability, which in itself may be enough, she also possesses the rarest of virtues."

"You mean her virginity?"

"That's not important. I mean that she attracts people. Her manner is infinitely touching and at the same time inspires obedience and respect."

"You could add veneration."

"She conquered us all even before opening her mouth. It would be a crime to let all those excellent qualities go to waste."

"What do you have in mind?"

"My idea is that she has what it takes to become a political success," cried the president excitedly, as he rose from his chair and began pacing the room with long strides. "My idea is that she's the type of woman I've been looking for and never found. I need such a woman in my administration, a woman whose dignified presence is so compelling that no one will challenge the reforms I plan to make. My idea is that she will be the gleaming torch of my government—it could use a bit of luster.

"Listen, my dear," he went on more calmly, "I'm counting on you to take good care of her, to educate her about our customs and the great problems we face—in short, to give her polish. I'm certain it won't take more than a few weeks. Then I'll offer her a government post—I'll create a special department for her if necessary, anything at all. Why not model it after your Association? Department of the Dignity of Women ... or simply Department of Women? That sounds fine and will suit her perfectly. Later on, perhaps, when she's broken in, we'll find something even more important for her to do."

"Unfortunately," observed Mme de Fonteneige, whose exhilaration was giving place to contemplation, "you won't be able to display her greatest claim to glory, for she's told us she wishes to remain incognito."

"That's to be expected, my dear. If I introduced her as the Virgin Mary I'd be taken for a madman or a charlatan. But it's easy to concoct a past for her— preferably a romantic one that excites curiosity and interest in her person. I'm counting on you for that too."

"What a shame!" sighed Mme de Fonteneige. "I was dying to introduce her to all my friends as the mother of God."

For a while longer the two of them went on savoring the hopes that Mary's coming had stirred insofar as their private interests were concerned and ended up forgetting the supernatural character of the event. Only at the last minute, as the president was about to leave, did Mme de Fonteneige recall the surprises revealed that evening. "By the way," she asked, "what do you think of this quarrel between the Father and the Son reported by the Holy Spirit?"

Dumont-Gayol smiled and gestured carelessly, then kissed her hand and replied as he walked out the door, "Shopkeepers' squabbles, my dear. I hope it all gets straightened out, of course, but I don't feel concerned in the least. There are too many other things on my mind."

○　　○　　○

After leaving the house, Father Routier and Reverend Roberts walked along through the darkness in silence, as if what they were thinking could not be put into words. "It's not possible," the priest declared suddenly. "I can't believe it. We all must have been hallucinating."

"Yet we saw her with our own eyes and touched her with our hands. I've always denounced this blind devotion to Mary as a fetishism—a point of contention between us, you know, for haven't you transformed her into a kind of pagan goddess? But as I looked at her I felt a compulsion to fall on my knees."

"I had the same urge," Routier admitted, "so I knelt too. I'm not certain whether I ought to feel ashamed or grateful for having witnessed a miracle."

"It has all the marks of a miracle. She materialized. She returned to earth a whole person as you claim she once departed it—a claim we've never recognized."

"Deep down, many of us Catholics have found it hard to accept," the priest confessed in a small voice.

"And the Spirit, what about him?" continued Roberts, now highly agitated. "How could we go on listening without a murmur to that outrageous story he told? That quarrel between...between...I haven't the courage to utter their names."

"I wanted to protest," Routier mumbled in a hollow voice. "I tried to put a stop to the blasphemy, to ward off what I took for an evil omen by making the sacred sign that is our weapon. Am I unworthy of my calling? Have I sinned by failing to recognize the divine breath? It was that very sign that drew him inside me: just as I made it he began to speak through my lips."

"The same thing happened to me. He forced my lips to say what he wanted. He didn't boast about it either. Routier, the Spirit has the power to control men's souls, everyone's soul, even a priest's!"

"We knew it!" Father Routier concluded, his voice barely above a whisper. "He breathes where he chooses. Now what's to become of us?"

VII

Marcole was thinking along quite different lines as he
made his way home alone—alone in appearance only,
for the Holy Ghost kept returning at intervals to haunt
him.

What had happened that evening had neither
puffed up his pride, as it did Mme de Fonteneige's,
nor inspired him with useful projects, nor sent him
into a panic of religious self-doubt. It had simply
sparked his curiosity, which was always on the alert
for unusual incidences of the behavior of matter. The
fact of being possessed by the Holy Spirit had thrown
him off balance at the start, but he quickly became

accustomed to it. This wasn't the first time he had felt affected by strange powers.

"To the extent of listening to one such power talking through your own lips without your knowledge and your being able to carry on a kind of dialogue together?" asked the Spirit, who was reading his thoughts.

"Not quite to that point, not aloud, if that's what you mean," replied Marcole, without batting an eyelash at this latest intrusion. "I must have been in a particularly receptive mood tonight, but I seem to recall having carried on a kind of inner dialogue with invisible beings on several occasions."

"Perhaps it was I conversing with you mentally without identifying myself," the Spirit suggested thoughtfully. "It's happened to me before. I believe I remember having had a few discussions with an out-of-the-ordinary and likable individual. I've only the vaguest recollection, however, for it was centuries before I became the Third Person of the Trinity. At that time I was known as either a guardian angel or a demon. As to the individual—a philosopher, I think— I've forgotten his name."

"Wasn't it Socrates?" asked Marcole, stopping abruptly at the curb.

"Socrates! That's it. You've heard of him?"

"Hasn't everybody? These dialogues don't surprise me, either on your part or his." The astrophysicist began walking again and talking, first in a monologue, then in rambling, amiable conversation.

"You're certainly a singular individual," the Spirit observed. "Nothing surprises you."

"Nothing surprises me?" Marcole puzzled over the statement for some time. Finally he admitted, "It's possible. As a matter of fact, everything fills me with wonder, but nothing surprises me."

"Not even seeing a woman materialize before your eyes in a Paris drawing room?"

"Not really."

"A woman—do forgive me if I occasionally read your thoughts; it's my one besetting sin—a woman whose history, according to the Church, has always struck you as a tale gracefully told?"

"I could be wrong. *Errare est humanum*. . . . Listen, Lord or demon, if I'm never surprised it's because I'm engaged in a profession where daily occurrences can be so strange that the apparition of a storybook character can't be considered an astounding phenomenon. I'm what is called down here an astrophysicist. I study celestial bodies by applying the latest techniques of physics—which means that I'm constantly dealing with the infinitely large and the infinitely small. I'm forever discovering mysteries next to which religions are insignificant."

"Is that so?" remarked the Spirit in a voice vibrant with curiosity. "Can you give me some examples?"

"I was still growing up when I learned that two events could both be and not be simultaneous, with the logical result that I could cease to grow older if I attained a certain speed."

• • • 57 • • •

"I don't see the relationship between those two phenomena. It disturbs me, for I like logic."

"I'll explain it to you someday if you have the patience to listen. . . . Later on, my teachers demonstrated that a corpuscle was capable of occupying two different positions at the same time. But all that was just trivia. . . . Do you know, Lord or demon," Marcole continued with growing excitement, "that in addition to the universe we can experience there are invisible worlds?"

"I'm well aware of that. . . ."

"Invisible both as to what is infinitely large and infinitely small. These worlds, which even retain the light, did you know we are beginning to define and analyze them? We'll never be able to penetrate them, but if it were possible, our precise calculations show that within their confines we could go back in time and relive the same events over again, the way a cyclist racing around a velodrome repeatedly passes in front of the same stands. Did you know that right in the center of enormous heaps of galaxies there probably exist mammoth astral bodies whose mass is five million times that of our sun?"

"Fantastic, I agree. I didn't know that, but I've always suspected unknown realms exist. I believe I'm the only one in heaven who can visualize such a possibility. But I'm here to learn, and hope this will be an educational experience for me while I'm among you."

"And you expect me to be astonished," Marcole

protested, having listened absent-mindedly, "by a woman's apparition tonight in the drawing room of Mme de Fonteneige!"

"This woman nevertheless is the Virgin Mary, mother of Christ," the Holy Spirit interrupted rather sharply. "You might have shown a tinge of emotion when I told you about the trouble in heaven!"

"You mean the dispute between Father and Son? I can understand, my dear demon—you don't mind my calling you that, do you? 'Lord' is too ceremonious."

"As you wish."

"I can understand, dear demon, that the situation is very significant for you and those around you up there. But these parochial wrangles have no bearing on my skies."

"Parochial!"

"Shopkeepers' squabbles, if you prefer."

"Strange," observed the Spirit meditatively, determined not to lose his temper, "just a while ago I dropped in at Mme de Fonteneige's place and heard President Dumont-Gayol use the same expression."

"He and I have entirely different concerns, but neither of us thinks about your paradise."

"You're lucky I'm not easily hurt."

"Don't assume that I'm totally callous. When you left me alone, I spent ten long minutes pondering that antagonism."

"Only ten minutes!"

"After which I put it out of mind forever, having

decided that this quarrel is a perfectly normal thing. Logical. Inevitable."

"Explain what you mean."

"I had always marveled at the feat engineered by the Christians when they united in a single entity two personalities as dissimilar as the Father and Son. In their haste to synthesize everything, they prodded the councils into forging a monstrous amalgam, which was bound to explode one day. Think about it, demon: on the one hand absolute power, harsh discipline bordering on cruelty, a tyrannical impulse; on the other, infinite goodness, mercy, forgiveness of sins, humility. That such a monster should devour itself doesn't astonish me at all."

"Only because I like you can I forgive you for this indifference. . . . But I'm curious to hear more about your sky. I didn't notice any of those peculiar features you mentioned when I traveled here through the ether."

"Ether!" Marcole snorted. "Ether never did exist. Every schoolboy since Einstein has known that."

"Space, if you like."

"More precisely, the spatio-temporal continuum."

"Don't parade learning that I'm in no position to verify. Can't you show me some image of this sky of yours? Though I'm pure spirit, I can still appreciate concrete representations. They often help one to comprehend ideas."

"We've reached my house. If you'll follow me into my study, I'll show you a map of the skies. It's one of the most advanced ones ever made. It will reveal worlds that exist millions of light-years away."

"Light-years?" the Spirit repeated quizzically.

"I'll explain it to you in stages, demon, just as I promised. Only don't interrupt me. I should tell you that even though this map gives a pretty accurate picture of the celestial bodies recorded by our instruments, it's no longer of great value to astrophysicists and I rarely consult it. What we're looking for is what remains hidden and to be discovered. But for you, dear demon, whose cleverness I'm just beginning to appreciate, it can serve as a convenient starting point. Don't be offended. I recognize that one can be a divinity and also hopelessly ignorant of what makes the universe tick."

"Your learning, friend, obliges me once more to excuse your conceit," grumbled the Holy Ghost. "Show me the map of your sky."

So it was that in Marcole's cluttered study filled with diagrams and graphs, equations scribbled all over notebooks, and scientific publications in many languages, the Holy Ghost, who had descended to resolve the problems of heaven, spent the rest of his first night peering at astronomical charts, asking question after question, and listening attentively to the scientist's patient explanations.

VIII

The days following that memorable séance were filled with frenetic activity for Mme de Fonteneige, who trotted out every weapon in her arsenal in order to launch the heaven-sent Madonna on the social waters and turn her into an illustrious earthling. This she had vowed to do the night of the apparition, and nothing could break her resolve.

Questions of dress, hairdo, and etiquette were quickly settled, thanks to her innate competence and a flair for exhorting her regular tradespeople to perform feats of heroism. Thanks also to Mary's cooperation and exceptional adaptability. Mary accepted orders from her mentor without a murmur and rarely made suggestions of her own, but when she did, they were delivered with firm authority learned from rubbing shoulders with members of the top celestial echelons.

"You really ought to have a suitable name, Holy Mother," Mme de Fonteneige advised her over a late breakfast the morning after her arrival. The mistress of the house had slept badly, tossing and turning for hours, yet had managed to whip together an active battle plan. "What would you say to 'Mary Queen'? I thought about it all night and couldn't come up with a name worthy of you that would also preserve your anonymity. Mary Queen seems to be the best answer."

"Mary Queen," the Virgin repeated. "Queen... Queen..." After a pause and a smile, she nodded. "I think that will be just fine. It lets me keep my first name, which I rather like, and 'Queen' isn't too bad."

Several days later Mme de Fonteneige presented Mary Queen to a select group of friends who made up the administrative committee of the Association for the Dignity of Women. True to the name it bore, this organization accepted only socially prominent ladies of impeccable dignity. Mme de Fonteneige had founded it in reprisal for the vulgarity and the outrageous behavior and speech of various feminist groups that offended her sense of decorum and, she felt, could only prove counterproductive.

Before introducing Mary, she had given her friends a thumbnail sketch of the personality Mary was to assume—the two of them having worked this out together after President Dumont-Gayol had blessed the scheme. Mary was to be French, of course, but brought up outside the country by a mother of foreign birth. Mme de Fonteneige padded out the scenario with thinly veiled allusions to a clandestine marriage between celebrities. Mary had been forced to live abroad until now, when conditions at last seemed right for her return.

While this hint of mystery fueled the curiosity of the Association's ladies, it also inspired certain misgivings, one of which was voiced by a baroness prior to Mary's appearance before the committee. "May I assume, my dear," said she, addressing her president, "that you have investigated Mlle Queen's moral character? These women who travel abroad are inclined to develop peculiar habits."

Mme de Fonteneige protested, explaining that she had known Mary Queen since childhood but could not elaborate further because her lips were sealed by a promise made long before. However, she could certainly attest to the high moral standards and unimpeachable conduct of Mary Queen and was prepared to swear to it on a stack of Bibles.

"My remark," observed the baroness, "was simply meant to remind us all that one of our unspoken rules is to exclude social climbers. However, since you attest to her sound moral fiber, my dear, I withdraw my objection."

When at last Mary entered the room, enveloped in this aura of mystery and the target of inquisitive stares, she stood her ground and managed not to appear too intimidated. Though the committee members were favorably impressed by her fine features and regal bearing, they still insisted she undergo the standard examination required of all applicants, and for which she had prepared under Mme de Fonteneige's tutelage. First she had to recite flawlessly from memory the lengthy "Declaration of the Rights of Women," a document painstakingly composed and solemnly promulgated by the committee, which had become the association's Bible.

Mary recited the text without a single slip, underscoring the principal passages with eloquent inflections that drew murmurs of approval. She had read the document the night before and digested it almost instantly. To her surprise, it wasn't boring and she felt strangely pleased to note that the virtues of women were exalted along with their indefensible rights and their place in the social order.

Each committee member then fired questions at her. Her pertinent answers displayed an intellect and wit as sharp as her memory. The fact that she lent herself to this inquisition with visible good humor apparently impressed some of her interrogators. With poise and tact she commented on every point, expressed informed opinions on the various problems facing the association, and evaded only indiscreet queries having to do with her mysterious origins— but again gracefully and with an irresistible smile. The committee voted unanimously to make her a member.

At the close of the meeting, Mme de Fonteneige accompanied each of her friends to the door and polled their reactions. Not once was she disappointed; the overall impression was excellent and highly flattering. Only the baroness, who wielded considerable influence with the committee, demonstrated a trace of uncertainty. "Very intelligent, to be sure," she commented. "Well-bred and distinguished, I should say. But is she Catholic? I don't believe you've informed us about the matter, which is of some significance if you plan, as I think you do, to give her important responsibilities on our committee."

"She is indeed," Mme de Fonteneige affirmed vigorously.

"Are you certain?"

"You have my word that she was baptized and is as good a Catholic as any of us."

"Practicing?"

"Naturally."

"Then let's take her," the baroness concluded. "I agree that she'll make an excellent recruit."

Remembering this conversation, Mme de Fonteneige did not fail to take Mary Queen to mass the following Sunday in the church she and several friends attended regularly. After instructing her protégée on what to do and how to do it during a ceremony about which the Virgin was totally ignorant and curious, she gave her a prayer book. As usual, Mary read and absorbed it instantly.

Mme de Fonteneige had no cause for concern that Mary's lack of religious training might produce an awful blunder. Paying not the slightest attention to the sea of prying eyes that followed her every move in church, Mary easily convinced the most devout souls of her piety. She made all the right responses, though she may have raised her voice a trifle too much in praise of the Holy Virgin and as the chorus intoned "Holy Mary, mother of God. . . ."

o   o   o

Relieved, Mme de Fonteneige turned her energies to launching Mary Queen in the capital. During the following week she took her to a number of social gatherings and introduced her to prominent persons in Paris literary and political circles. Wherever she went Mary drew curious stares at first, then a warm and enthusiastic reception. By spreading rumors and fueling the mystery of her protégée's secret past, Mme de Fonteneige managed to focus attention on her, which attention Mary maintained by her radiant personality and the prodigious knowledge she had acquired in just a few days. She used this knowledge artfully and with such tact and modesty that in a matter of weeks she had become the toast of society.

So as not to waste a moment, Mme de Fonteneige gave a small dinner party and invited a close friend and adviser of President Dumont-Gayol. After observing the rising star very closely, he subjected her to a second rigorous inquisition from which once again she emerged victorious. Her replies demonstrated that there was nothing she didn't know about high-level politics or analyzing and solving problems.

The adviser gave an extremely flattering report on her to the president, who had already decided to offer Mary a job when Mme de Fonteneige, whose advice he valued, declared, "My instincts tell me she's just the woman you need. You know that I rarely make mistakes when it comes to judging competency. Give her a top-level position and you'll never regret it. She's a born politician with the face of a Madonna."

So it happened that several weeks later Mary was offered the chance to run the Ministry of Women, a post created just for her and which she accepted with the dignified restraint that had become her hallmark.

IX

Shortly afterward, the Holy Spirit left the earth and returned to report on his mission to the Father in heaven. He found him sitting alone on a throne that radiated ever so faintly, surrounded by a court reduced to a handful of loyal archangels, the eldest of the celestial community, he noted, and somewhat the worse for wear.

"That's the way it is," sighed the Father wearily. "The Son has left me. The place at my right hand wasn't good enough for him anymore. At first he went over and sat on my left, which for some reason appealed to him as the nobler side. I let him do it, but even that didn't seem to satisfy his overwhelming ambition. The next thing I knew, he had the audacity to demand that we take turns sitting on *my* supreme throne. Naturally I refused, presuming that before long he would try to oust me altogether. So he left and went off to occupy a neighboring throne. Unfortunately, a procession of saints and angels followed him to form the nucleus of a new and expanding court. You find me humiliated and depressed, and I doubt that the news you bring from earth will be of much comfort. I've heard advance rumors."

"No, Lord, the news isn't good," said the Spirit, who had all he could do not to weep at the run-down state of the once glorious palace. "Inducing the change will be a slow and difficult process if, in fact, we can manage to do it. Up to now I've made only fragile contacts: the human beings I've successfully possessed listen to me when I'm inside them and revert to their old bad habits the minute I've left—a body of beliefs built up by the councils over twenty centuries that is tough to breach. Still, I hope to make some progress in time, but, as I say, it will be slow going. I can't hide the fact, Lord, that at this moment the Son is outdistancing you."

"Why try to hide it from me?" the Father exclaimed bitterly. "I'm all too aware of it. If the Son is determined to raise a storm by deserting my throne, it's because he's been encouraged by the flood of prayers from below, prayers that, for the most part, ignore me. I believe he opted for this latest act of defiance shortly after the new pope's election."

"You know about that, Lord? I intended to fill you in on the details of this unfortunate incident."

"I've heard rumors, but they're enough to make me ill. Since you've just come from there, you needn't spare my feelings."

"I was in Rome, Lord, and had succeeded in possessing, on and off, in the face of stubborn resistance, the soul of a priest with considerable influence at the Vatican, one Father Routier. With some of his colleagues, we were awaiting the results of the conclave in one of the palace rooms. Now and then I would drop a comment calculated to enlarge your image— carefully worded, of course, for as I've told you, very few of them are prepared to renounce their beliefs. Like the rest of the crowd, we kept our eyes glued to the chimney, watching for the smoke to rise..."

"A large crowd, I presume?"

"Several hundred thousand. We saw black smoke rise a number of times."

"Come to the point, please. None of this means anything to me."

"After waiting one whole day, we finally saw a plume of white smoke. I'll skip the official announcements and tell you what the new pontiff said in his first public appearance."

"He spoke?"

"He said in Italian, *'Sia laudato Jesu Christo!'*

May Jesus Christ be praised! Those were his first words."

"That's what I heard," sighed the Father. "How did people react?"

"I've never witnessed such wild applause. Then he said something else, Lord, but I'm not sure I should tell you. It's very significant."

"Tell me. I might as well drain my poisoned cup down to the last bitter dregs."

"Well, Lord, he said, 'I dreaded the thought of my election to this office, but I accepted it out of obedience to Jesus Christ and confidence in the Holy Virgin.'"

"Now it's the Virgin!" the Father exploded. "What's Mary got to do with this? Didn't he even utter the name of his maker?"

"Only at the end, Lord, and I must admit that I had something to do with it. Having left Father Routier when the pope began speaking, I tried to penetrate him and make him pay homage to the God he seemed to have forgotten. He put up stiffer resistance than all the other priests. The mere mention of the Son—the Mother, too, incidentally—left him spellbound, I noticed. I was lucky to get him to pronounce your name twice, although not in the most acceptable manner. First he said, 'I am introducing myself to all of you so that we may confess our common faith in the mother of God and of the Church.'"

"The mother again!" roared the Lord. "And what about the Father?"

"I've told you that he wasn't obeying my directions very well. He ended up saying, 'Let us begin to go forward again along the path of history and of the Church, with the help of God'—you see, he did mention you twice!—'and of mankind.'"

"The help of God and mankind!" moaned the Father. "Lumped together! Some consolation!"

"That's all I could get out of him. A few days later he gave another speech along the same lines and I couldn't make him budge. He said, 'O Christ, let me become and remain a servant of your sole power....'"

"Your sole power!" the Father shouted. "That's the limit!"

"There's no purpose in my reciting the rest of his sermon, Lord. Suffice it to say that the Son's name occurred seven times, but not once did I hear yours, Father. I tell you this simply to illustrate the religious mentality of the so-called faithful. In their eyes, you're playing second fiddle. Let's face it."

"I guess we have to face it," the Father conceded, heaving a deep sigh. "This rupture has been infecting Western civilization for close to twenty centuries.... Do you still feel there's some chance, with time and patience, of making these heathen see the light? *You* at least aren't taken in by their self-deception, are you? Maybe they'll wind up persuading even you that you're God! I worry about this sometimes."

"Lord, you know that I've no ambition. All I want is for the truth to come out, and absolute divine unity seems closer to the truth than any Trinity. That's my belief and that's why I continue to serve you.

"Also, in my travels I've run into some intelligent individuals, both religious and nonreligious, who have a habit of asking questions. Quite a few among them have been influenced by a Jesuit priest considered something of a heretic in his day by orthodox Christians, but whose posthumously published writings seem to have impressed certain theologians. I've read everything Father Teilhard de Chardin has written and learned some very interesting things."

"Really?"

"Alas, Lord, there you are dispossessed too, for though the good father believes the world is progressing toward unification with the divine, the divine is still represented by the Son. Of course, being a Jesuit, he couldn't very well—"

"The Son! Always the Son!" groaned the Father. "Have the pope, the priesthood, and everyone else forgotten my supreme commandment: Thou shalt have no other gods before me?"

"You have to put yourself in their shoes and forgive them, Lord," observed the Spirit, objective and conciliatory as ever. "To them, the Son is God just as you are God. That Nicean heresy persists and is the basis of this unfortunate *quid pro quo*, which I'm doing my best to correct, believe me.

"Even if I haven't yet induced the persons I've contacted to admit their errors, at least I've got some of them to agree to meet and exchange ideas. Eminent spokesmen of various sects will attend, each presenting his concept of divine power. I'm very hopeful that a clearer image will result. Anyway, it will provide a helpful source of information."

"And where will this meeting take place?"

"At the astrophysicist Marcole's place. He's a scientist and a materialist whose ideas are quite different from ours, but he has his own kind of religion and thinks about things that interest me. We've struck up a friendship and he's agreed to host a cocktail party and invite these other people."

"A cocktail party?"

"That's the pretext for people getting together to exchange ideas, something like the banquets of ancient times. Everyone on the list has accepted, for they know I'll be there and each is convinced his own convictions will prevail. I, for one, hope that eternal truth will outrun them all."

"So do I," murmured the Father. . . . "And what about Mary?" he added after a pause.

"I think Mary will turn out to be a powerful ally in your cause, Lord, because she's becoming a national figure in France. She's carving herself a brilliant career down there."

"Really?" muttered the Father. "I wouldn't have thought her up to it."

"You wouldn't recognize her, Lord. She holds a high office that gives her considerable influence, especially over women, who are generally more concerned than men with religious matters. She's on her own now. I haven't visited her lately, having had too much to do myself. I'm certain she'll succeed in promoting our views. She has one great advantage over me: a body, a physical presence."

"Attractive?"

"Irresistible. Her public appearances have been an enormous success. I must say, she looks radiant. Earth's climate seems to agree with her; she's lost that wan complexion that used to make her look so glum up here. She seems very happy with her new job and is quite in command. The fervent support for her is reflected in the polls, the latest of which gave her sixty percent of the vote—a rarity on earth."

"Rarer still in heaven!" moaned the Father.

The two went on talking for a while, after which the Holy Spirit left, unable to dispel the worried frown on the divine brow. Depressed by the dismal gloom of the throne room, the Spirit felt a great sense of relief as he stepped out of the palace and cast one last look at the venerable archangels, who seemed to totter a bit as they sank to their knees.

> "Pitifully trailing their great white wings
> Like oars alongside..."[1]

he murmured as he went on his way. In the past he had mingled with poets too.

[1] Charles Bandelaire, "The Albatross" in *The Flowers of Evil*.

PART TWO

THE COCKTAIL PARTY

I

Marcole greeted his guests and seated them in easy chairs he had borrowed for the evening, since the simple, informal furnishings in his apartment were none too comfortable. The room in which he held the party served for entertaining, working, and, when he was involved in some all-absorbing project, eating. He had spent the whole day tidying up the place, although his small group of guests had no relish for luxurious surroundings. Still, knowing the discussion would probably continue late into the night, he felt he ought to provide at least a minimum of bodily comforts.

The man in the white jacket—also on loan for the evening—delivered to each guest the drink of his choice and a plate of canapés. The astrophysicist then rose and the Holy Spirit inside him spoke. "Gentlemen and good friends, thank you for coming at Marcole's invitation and my request. You know that we are gathered here to examine and compare ideas, which I will find most valuable. I propose that we imitate the guests of Agathon[1] at a banquet of his I recall having attended long, long ago, and that we, like they, choose the loftiest subject of debate. For them it was Eros, god of love; for you and me, I think it is the nature of divinity, particularly the Trinity, which interests most of you whether or not you choose to worship it."

There was no objection to this proposal, only murmurs of assent. The guests had been forewarned of the supernatural powers claimed by the speaker.

"The excellence of our present company," continued the Spirit, "laymen and clergy alike, befits our making speeches in honor of divinity. Since the subject is agreeable to you, it should inspire our tongues. We could imitate the guests at that ancient banquet and each of us in turn, going from left to right, discourse nobly and wisely. Father Routier, on my left, will speak first, which is justified by his calling, and

[1]Athenian dramatist (c.450-c.400 B.C.) The setting of Plato's *Symposium* is a banquet at Agathon's house (Trans.).

my friend Marcole, whose person you must excuse me for having borrowed temporarily, will be last. Does this suit you?"

"Fine by me," replied Marcole in his normal voice. "But why do you insist on talking like Plato, who narrates the banquet scene? Are you so attached to the past?"

"Not really. It is only that I admired his style and never forgot it."

"There's not a trace of Socrates in me except his ugly face, and your suggestion that I speak last isn't exactly an advantage. Still, I hope to learn something from all the wise opinions I will have listened to."

"It's all right by me too, dear Eryximachus..." Father Routier began. From the moment he had seen the Holy Spirit manifest itself and the Virgin materialize, his life had become utter confusion, yet he mustered his considerable mental resources and, bolstered by burning faith, resolved to keep his sanity. Later on, whenever the Third Person harassed him, he usually succeeded in prying himself loose. He persisted in thinking he had fallen victim to an illusion that would vanish in time. Not one to run from adversity, and intent on his mission to keep informed about everything, Routier had agreed to take part in this evening's activities. His sense of humor fortified him during this critical period and gave him a feeling for how the coming debate would unfold. Knowing the Greek classics as well as the Bible, he took up the challenge of a seemingly harmless sport and replied, smiling, "It's all right by me too, dear Eryximachus, but I'm not Phaedrus and I don't feel up to delivering a lengthy discourse. I've come here only to assert my convictions, and you all know what they are."

Reverend Roberts, who was there for the same purpose as his Catholic colleague, asked a question. "Before we begin our speeches, which inspire you with such confidence and I don't oppose, I'd like to ask whether you intend to intervene in your usual manner. By that I mean your penetrating each of us in turn, trying to impose your will and forcing us to voice your ideas. That doesn't strike me as fair play."

"Thus pouring the wisdom of an overflowing mind into an empty soul, as one transfers water from a full vase into an empty one,[1]" the astrophysicist recited, having also read a classic or two in his day.

"My dear Marcole," replied the Spirit, "you're not Socrates but you express yourself as he did. Rest easy, and you, reverend, don't worry. As you put it, it wouldn't be fair play on my part to foul up the game. I've come this evening to hear what you have to say and to try to form my own opinion. Actually, it's one of my favorite diversions: listening to a number of conflicting points of view. I'll content myself with the role of discussion leader and won't try to influence you. If I say anything at all, I'll say it through the lips

[1]Plato, *The Banquet*

of my friend Marcole and you'll know I'm speaking for myself. Does this satisfy you?"

"I suppose so," the reverend replied.

"May I also have the privilege of asking a question?" inquired Shi-Peng, a young Chinese Marxist doctor of philosophy invited by Marcole at the request of the Spirit, who was eager for confrontations between radically different points of view.

"Please do."

"Discoursing by turns is all very well and good, but are we allowed to interrupt the speaker? A series of questions and answers may get to the truth faster than a long speech."

"That sounds reasonable to me," said the Spirit. "Agreed. . . . One more thing: I'd like to apologize for these abominable chairs. Couches would have been more appropriate, but Marcole objected that they would only confuse and disorient everyone. We also decided against inviting flute-girls to entertain you and delight your senses. No doubt the clergy among us would not have appreciated the thought."

"For my part," politely observed Dr. Ahmrad, one of the guests and a noted expert on the Muslim religion, "I would not have objected to such attractions, although I don't find them indispensable."

"In any event, dancing and music would not have contributed a single crumb of wisdom to our discussions," added Rabbi Klein, an authority on Jewish law, with a twinkle in his eye.

"Well spoken," the Spirit noted. "On the other hand, my friend Marcole has spared nothing to provide us with excellent food and drink. I reminded him of what Xenophon's Socrates said at another banquet: *Friends, I urge us to drink; like the mandrake root that drugs the body, wine, which refreshes the spirit, lightens our sorrows; it arouses joy like oil stirring up the flames.*[1] I trust, father," he added, addressing Routier, "that this bodily nourishment, which unfortunately I can't taste, won't offend you, and now I invite you to take the floor."

Father Routier nodded approvingly, drank heartily from his glass of champagne, and began.

[1]Xenophon, *Banquet II*

II

FATHER ROUTIER'S DISCOURSE

"I don't despise the fruits of the earth, my dear Marcole, (forgive me, Lord, if it was really you speaking, but I don't think it was) and I like your wine, which I drink temperately according to the precepts of Socrates, whom you just quoted in part only. Allow me to complete the statement he made at the banquet described in Xenophon: *Our bodies are like seeds that sprout in the soil. When too much rain falls, they have trouble growing ... but if watered moderately, they flourish. ... In the same way, if we drink to excess, the body staggers, the spirit flags, and, unable to utter a word, we can barely breathe.* So I shall limit myself to one or two cups of this nectar.

"My speech will probably disappoint you; this I regret. But just as the spirit flags if we drink to excess, so do I hold that an overabundance of words clouds the understanding. Frankly, and with all due apologies to Dr. Shi-Peng, I don't believe that knowledge springs from dialectics."

The Chinese philosopher smiled and acknowledged the comment with a friendly gesture.

"I prefer to concentrate on a few premises proven and re-proven since the coming of Christ and that I hold to be eternal truths."

"What you call 'proven,' father," interrupted Shi-Peng, "actually means validated by theologians after endless debate. And isn't that a kind of dialectic?"

"You may be right, my son, but there is a time for everything: time for discussion and time for faith. I have reached the time for faith and now wish to sum up the eternal certainties that constitute my convictions. There is a God and only one, beyond a doubt, but this single God is divided into three separate persons—the separateness is also an established truth. These three persons are the Father, creator of everything that exists; the Son, saviour who became embodied in man in order to redeem his original sin; and the Spirit, who inhabits our souls and through his divine substance unites us with God. I should add that it is inconceivable for any rivalry to occur among these three persons or between the first two for the simple reason that they are but one God."

"Forgive me, Routier, for interrupting in turn," Marcole spoke out in his normal voice, "but these statements are practically incoherent. You never would have made them when we were both studying mathematics. I've told you this a thousand times and I can't help repeating it once more."

The priest ignored the interruption and continued. "This story about a quarrel is tantamount to blasphemy. However, I take it as a joke—tasteless, to be sure, and unlikely to heap honors on its author—that keeps me from getting too upset."

Having said this, Father Routier eyed Marcole uneasily, but the Holy Spirit kept his word and did not try to possess him and force him to deny his beliefs as the priest feared he might.

"That's fine," the Spirit commented briefly, still speaking through the astrophysicist. "Thank you, father, for presenting your credo so candidly, even if it doesn't satisfy lovers of pure logic like my friend Marcole. I'll even forgive your suspicions about me, having been in doubt too often myself to take offense. If nobody has any comments to make, Reverend Roberts will be the next speaker."

"I think you ought to skip me, Lord," said the minister. "Not that I don't find the discussion interesting, for I do, but I would only repeat what Father Routier has just said. Essentially, we share the same faith. The differences between us are of concern only to theological experts and would bore you. If you don't mind, I'll give up my turn to Rabbi Klein, an eminent scholar of Jewish law, which I don't approve of but I do respect."

RABBI KLEIN'S DISCOURSE

"Father Routier and Reverend Roberts won't hold it against me if I take issue with them over the doctrine of the Trinity, which I find utterly irrational, as someone already pointed out, and therefore untenable. I believe in a single God who would never, under any circumstances, transform himself into two separate persons, much less three. This transcendent deity, creator of all things in six stages, cannot have had a son, and the designation of Holy Spirit is understood to be one of his attributes. . . . I see that you have a question, Dr. Shi-Peng."

"Excuse me, Dr. Klein," said the Marxist philosopher, who had raised one finger. "I shall take advantage of the fact that we are permitted to ask questions. I have no expert knowledge of Western religions, but it seems to me that your God, the God of the Jews, is the same as the Christian God—yours, father, and yours, reverend—since he is the God of the Old Testament whom you all take for the truth revealed."

"He probably is," Father Routier admitted rather testily after a short pause.

"If I wanted to be controversial," continued Rabbi Klein, "I'd insinuate that you took possession of Yahweh in order to turn him into one of those monstrous pagan divinities so dear to the Greeks. This strikes me as a step backward in the history of religious development."

"We do understand your point of view, rabbi," the Spirit interjected just as the two clerics were about to protest, "but in your faith what becomes of the person known to Christians as the Son, who is assuredly an important personage in paradise?"

"Before answering you, whoever you are, angel or phantom, I should like to present a few quotations. Here is one: *Love one another from the bottom of your heart, and if a man sin against you, speak gently to him and bear him no malice.*"

Appeased, Father Routier said, "My dear rabbi, I'm delighted to hear you preaching the Gospel. I felt sure we'd discover a common ground of understanding."

"And now this: *Love the Lord and thy fellow man. Worship the Lord all thy life, and love one another with a sincere heart.*"

Ignoring a warning signal from Reverend Roberts, who was trying to restrain him, Father Routier never heard the words, "Look out! It's a trap!" that the pastor whispered in his ear. He replied with characteristic zeal, "That's in *Matthew*, chapter twenty-three, verse thirty-seven or thirty-nine, if I'm not mistaken..."

Nor did he hear the pastor's second whispered protest, "Nonsense! It's in the Encyclopedia Britannica!" as he continued, "The quotation may not be exact but that's the sense of it. I couldn't be happier, rabbi, to see that you attach sufficient importance to Christ's teachings for you to memorize them."

"Thank you, father, but there's a slight difference of opinion. The author of those admirable words happens to be a Jew who lived a hundred and nine or a hundred and seven years before your Christ, a Jewish pharisee to boot. You'll find those passages and others in a document entitled 'Testament of the Twelve Patriarchs.'"

"I believe you," murmured Routier a bit sheepishly. "What does it prove?"

"Simply that Jesus Christ actively preached a current trend of thinking that others long before him had expressed, including the pharisees whom he reviled. ... It might be a good idea to re-examine what he accused them of: hypocrisy and pride. Not all of them were like that, but then we would have to..."

"Please, rabbi," the Holy Spirit intervened, "our subject is the nature of God. You don't look upon Jesus Christ as God?"

"This we cannot do, but that's no fault of his, since he never used the designation on earth. No, our quarrel is with his more or less well-meaning converts who formulated illogical theories he knew nothing about, such as the Redemption, the Incarnation, and the Trinity. If we ignore these outlandish trappings that reek of paganism, we are prepared to acknowledge Christ as a man of lofty morality, even if he tended to interpret the Torah in his own peculiar fashion.

"There is much more I could say about our faith, but I think I've presented the essentials as far as this meeting is concerned. The rest, as Reverend Roberts said, I'll leave to the experts. I hope I haven't hurt anyone's feelings, and now I yield the floor to the learned Muslim, Dr. Ahmrad, who sits at my left. He will undoubtedly favor us with some astute observations that I look forward to hearing."

DR. AHMRAD'S DISCOURSE

"As to the nature of divine power," the scholar began, "the Mohammedans see eye to eye with you, Dr. Klein, on at least one point: the absolute unity of God, whom we call Allah. Let me start by affirming that unity, which evidently conflicts with the concept of three separate persons endorsed by the reverend fathers, whose forbearance I ask."

"I see that we're outnumbered here," grumbled Routier.

"You forget me," said the Holy Spirit. "For the present, at least, I'm obliged to believe in three separate persons."

"A single God, then," Ahmrad continued, "who created the world in six days and revealed himself to mankind through the prophets. To some of these prophets he presented a book; to Moses he gave the Torah; to Jesus..."

Shi-Peng, whose face registered the most fascination of anyone by what he had just heard, raised a finger timidly and excused himself once again for interrupting. "This is highly impertinent, I realize, but I've just had such a remarkable thought that I can't keep it to myself any longer. Your God, Dr. Ahmrad, and yours, Dr. Klein, is also the God of the Bible. So you worship the same God?"

"That's one way of looking at it," the rabbi acknowledged after a moment's reflection.

"And this God, reverend fathers, is also the Christian God, the same divinity who inspired the Old Testament, which you regard as holy writ—you admitted it a moment ago. This, gentlemen, strikes me as altogether miraculous."

Father Routier cast a puzzled look at the Chinese as if suspicious that the Holy Spirit's meddling lay behind this interruption. But the Spirit spoke out eagerly through Marcole's lips, saying, "I must confess that it impresses me as miraculous, too. Father, how wrong you were to underestimate the efficacy of dialectics. There's nothing like this kind of open discussion to bring out truths—truths hidden since the world began, as one of your philosophers modestly puts it. And why are they hidden? Perhaps because they're too obvious."

After thinking about this, the expert on Mohammedan law admitted he had never realized this quite so clearly and proceeded with his discourse. "So to Moses he gave the Torah, to Jesus the Scriptures."

"Then you admit a connection between Jesus and divine authority?"

"A connection, certainly. Jesus was a prophet and a great one. Like all prophets, he was visited by the divine spirit, but he was not divine. And don't think that the mystery of his birth, as Christians see it, offends us. One miracle more or less hardly matters and we readily acknowledge the virginity of Mary.

"One of our important tenets concerning Jesus is that he did not die on the cross as everyone seems to think. Certain Gnostics had foreseen this truth and Mohammed confirmed it. We cannot conceive of his dying thus; actually, a substitution was made. The real Christ, the prophet, inspired by the breath of God, was not crucified. Shortly before the Passion, he abandoned his double and was transported to heaven by angels. This double, a phantom who looked just like him, was put to death instead, which explains his moaning, 'My God, my God, why has thou forsaken me?'"

"A phantom!" protested Father Routier, crossing himself.

"A phantom!" Reverend Roberts stammered vacuously.

"A phantom, really," murmured the Spirit meditatively.

During the long pause that followed, every guest seemed buried in thought. Then Dr. Ahmrad resumed his discourse, saying, "A phantom. That is an article of our faith. The real Jesus was a prophet. Mohammed was another one, the last of the line and, if I may be so bold, the greatest, because he built upon and perfected the wisdom of all the others. And that, gentlemen, sums up what I have to say on the subject of divinity. The rest—our heaven, our hell, our angels— is all very familiar to you and I shan't bother to dwell on it.

"Let me conclude by insisting on this one crucial point that seems to trouble all of you, while to us it is self-evident: the real Jesus was never crucified; his double was. You must realize, reverend," he continued, plainly directing his words to Roberts, "that we have great respect for prophets, we Muslims. To us, a prophet is like a lord—you would call him a gentleman, I think—and it has always amazed and disheartened me that any British subject could be naïve enough to imagine a gentleman being put to such a degrading and repulsive form of torture as crucifixion."

Reverend Roberts turned scarlet. He opened his mouth to protest, then changed his mind, shrugged his shoulders, and retreated into a brooding silence.

III

At Marcole's suggestion, the guests took a breather and exchanged polite conversation while the bartender refilled their glasses. When the man in the white jacket had gone back behind his table, the Holy Spirit thanked the first speakers again and turned to one of the few remaining guests who had yet to say anything. He was a well-known young author of novels and essays, deeply religious and devoutly Catholic. A number of his books proclaimed his intensely Christian outlook, but his unorthodox concept of Christ caused dismay in traditional circles.

"Now it's our friend Martial's turn to speak. I look forward, as I'm sure all of you do, to hearing the religious convictions of our younger generation, or at least a particular religious trend that has gained public notice. Is M. Martial prepared to instruct and delight us?"

Martial declared that he was ready, but the Chinese Shi-Peng interrupted once again with a string of apologies. "Dear friends," he said, "it will be my turn to take the floor after the present speaker, but a long statement by me on the heels of such eloquent presentations would appear dull and boring. Furthermore, my beliefs have much in common with those of M. Martial. I know he doesn't agree, but that's the way I see it. So I humbly request that we dispense with my discourse and you let me interrupt his speech from time to time, more often than I've done so far."

After Martial and the other guests had signaled their approval, the spokesman for avant-garde Christian ideology began.

MARTIAL'S DISCOURSE

"You know," he said, turning to Father Routier, "that I'm a devout Christian. Though a layman, my faith, you may be sure, is as strong as yours. Christ—for Christ is our central concern today—is a prodigious divinity to me, the supreme divinity. But something unusual for a religious-minded person happened to me—accidentally I presume. I'm aware of scientific progress; I've done a lot of thinking about the scientific discoveries of the past few centuries. It was a long, hard struggle for me to reconcile these two tendencies and come up with a rational synthesis. I can sum up the result of this synthesis in two statements, both of which express nearly the same conviction. The first is a quotation from Professor Haldane: *If the cooperation of several thousand million brain cells can produce our brain power, the idea becomes vastly more plausible that the cooperation of mankind, or a fraction of it, determines what Comte called a great superhuman being.*[1]

"The other is an assertion by Father Teilhard de Chardin, my mentor: *One great family, the kingdom of God? Yes, in a sense, but in another sense also a prodigious biological operation—that of the redemptive Incarnation.*"[2]

"Biological operation!" protested Father Routier. "I and my church are willing to concede a few points of theory to that Jesuit, but his language is more than I can stomach."

[1] J.B.S. Haldane, *The Inequality of Man and Other Essays*, 1932
[2] Teilhard de Chardin, *The Phenomenon of Man*, 1959

"A prodigious biological operation," the Chinese philosopher repeated in turn. "More and more, dear M. Martial, I'm coming to believe that we think alike on a number of topics. I agree with you entirely about the biological operation, though not about the re-demptive Incarnation of Christ. Let me mention a lecture delivered by Professor Samuel Alexander that is like a breviary to me. My memory is not as keen as yours and I can't quote any passage verbatim, but in substance, this is his conclusion: It's not God who created the world, but the world, which, slowly and patiently since the beginning of time, has been work-ing to create a God."[1]

"Well spoken," the Spirit responded approvingly. "So now friends, your similarities and differences are clearly defined."

"Regarding our differences," Martial continued, "I notice that you did not mention one aspect of Teil-hard's work: I mean the admirable synthesis by which he reconciles Christianity and science."

"A poor example of synthesis," retorted Shi-Peng, "that strikes me as the central lameness of his philos-ophy. Whether due to timidity or not, it demonstrates a lack of intellectual rigor—as some of his critics note, who impute it to his service in a religious order that . . ."

"Before you go on," the Spirit interrupted, "may

---

[1]Professor Samuel Alexander, *Space, Time and Deity* (Gifford Lec-tures), 1920

I express a slightly different attitude toward the work of this priest. I began reading his books when I came down to earth. I studied them during the hours I inhabited the body of my learned friend Marcole, who once was impressed by them but now considers them outmoded."

"Do go on, Lord," the two philosophers urged. "The evening is young, and it would be a mistake to neglect the views of the Spirit among spirits."

"Well then, for you, Martial, it's a marvelous synthesis; for you, Shi-Peng, a manifestation of Jesuitism, with all the pejorative overtones that term implies. You didn't use the word, but it's in your head, I know. I'd like to propose a finer distinction. The synthesizing effort in Teilhard's work impressed me as a splendid artistic production that deserves applause. To succeed by talent, by artistry—there's no other word for it— in juxtaposing two such contradictory currents of thought as Christianity and the science of evolution; to give a reasonable appearance of logic to a single theory combining the rational and the irrational, discipline and dream: this is an intellectual masterpiece, the product of a mind that strains and twists as it seeks out the impossible answer to a preposterous problem and winds up creating this patchwork solution in a flash of genius. A feat similar to, but even more prodigious than the association in one God of two persons as unlike as the Father and the Son. Marvelous synthesis indeed, but chiefly a literary monument, and I can understand why you, a writer of fiction, appreciate its true merits. Boundless creative imagination. That's all I have to say. Sorry for the digression."

"Lord," Shi-Peng remarked with a smile, "after contemplating what you have said, I wonder if your amazement isn't more akin to my reservation than to M. Martial's admiration."

"I share your observation," muttered Father Routier. "What's more, I didn't detect the verbal style of the one who calls himself Spirit and I wonder if he really spoke or if it was you, Marcole, who excel at propounding eccentric statements without letting on whether you're joking or dead serious."

"In other words, is it Socrates or his demon?" said the smiling mouth of the astrophysicist. "I'm not sure myself. We're getting so used to each other that sometimes we get mixed up. It doesn't matter. Close parenthesis and please go on, Martial."

"To return to the person who interests us most particularly tonight, I, like my mentor, believe in two totally different Christs—"

"Oh!" gasped the Holy Spirit. This time it was perfectly clear that he had made the exclamation. He apologized promptly. "Go on, Martial. I'll explain later the reason for my surprise—another musty memory."

"So we have two different Christs. The first is the historical Christ, who walked among us nearly twenty centuries ago, because history had to have a beginning—actually not a beginning, for the Incarnation

• • • 101 • • •

started well before the formation of atoms and the organization of chaos; not a beginning but a stage in the penetration of nature by divine power. The second is the universal Christ, the cosmic Christ, the pole that gradually becomes incorporated into the universe and transforms it into itself."

"That's the reason for my astonishment," the Spirit broke in. "Two Christs, you said? Oddly enough, that reminds me of what Pausanias said at the banquet described by Plato. Speaking of love, Pausanias said: There are two Erotes, the divine Eros and the earthly Eros. I can't help drawing a parallel between your cosmic Christ and your historical one. But I'm concerned with the historical or earthly Christ. May I ask which of the two inspires your worship?"

"How can you ask such a question, Lord?" Martial said impatiently. "The two cannot be compared. Father Teilhard put it this way: *What I and every creature cry out for, with every fiber of my being and of my earthly passion, is something quite different from a comrade to cherish: it is a God to worship.*"[1]

"Surely through inadvertence you omitted to quote the beginning of the sentence," Shi-Peng interjected benevolently. *"What should we ask of the Judea of two thousand years ago?* Indeed, what should we ask?"

[1]Teilhard de Chardin, *The Divine Milieu: an Essay on the Interior Life*

"I see that you're as familiar as I with the good father's writings. But don't try to drag him into your camp. We may share certain views, but we also have a fundamental difference. For me, I respeat, the biological operation is an ongoing incarnation."

"And for me, a nonstop creation. That doesn't detract from my admiration for your mentor. With just an ounce of courage he might have gone a step farther. Take away his earthly Christ—he calls him historical—and the God of the future, in whom we believe, remains to be created by mankind. We are accommodating, and as regards your last point, we don't mind too much your baptizing him Christ if that's what you want. Words are less important than ideas. As for the other one, the man of Galilee, he's disappearing in the mists of time, like a phantom."

"Another phantom!" exclaimed Reverend Roberts.

"I don't want to hear any more about phantoms," Father Routier whimpered.

"Phantom..." the Spirit repeated dreamily, "but that's something I still have to deal with."

There was another pause, as if the mention of a phantom had an inhibiting effect on the guests. Then Martial concluded, saying, "I think I've covered all the important points. I've spoken honestly and hope I didn't offend anyone, neither you, reverend fathers, who remain so attached to the historical Christ, nor you, Shi-Peng, who eliminate him."

IV

The Holy Spirit thanked the last speaker on behalf of everyone and paused briefly before addressing the occupant of the next seat, a tall man named Moos, whose age was hard to tell. His flowing beard and his dreamy gaze focused on the horizon gave him the appearance of a magus. Born in Eastern Europe, he had been living in France for many years. This self-taught intellectual had no titles or degrees and spent his nights pouring over all kinds of texts, from the cabala to the latest scientific treatises. He, too, had not said a word since the meeting began. "According to our rules, it's your turn to speak, Moos," said the Spirit. "I'm eager to hear your religious beliefs; from what I'm told, they're well worth our attention."

MOOS'S DISCOURSE

"Friends, don't take offense if my conception of your divinity is nothing like yours. Yours are based on what Christian, Jewish, and Mohammedan scholars regard as holy writ, but long and patient study of these documents has led me to conclusions totally unrelated to theirs.

"The earth was not created by Yahweh, whom Christians falsely name the Father and who was not the eternal and almighty God that some naïve exegetes proclaimed after a very superficial reading of the Scriptures. It was settled by creatures from a remote planet about twenty thousand years ago, creatures far superior to the primitive race then inhabiting our own planet, indeed, even more highly civilized than we are today, but who were not divine except in the simple minds of those who watched them descending from the sky."

"You mean cosmonauts?" Marcole asked.

"That's their modern name, but in the Bible

they're called elohims, or angels, or, when it's a matter of identifying the leader or leaders of the expedition, we find the names: Yahweh, Adonai, and Shaddai, among others.

"I ought to mention that long before we made scientific studies of the sacred texts, a group of Gnostic sects, namely Ophites, showed good judgment in refusing to recognize them as gods. They called them demiurges, which, while not exact, is closer to the truth. The Ophites visualized Yahweh as a jealous and arrogant demiurge called Ialdabaoth, whose fictitious skirmishes with the angels—rivals of his or perhaps rebellious underlings—are recounted by Anatole France. Basilides named one of these leaders Archon and described him as wise, kind, and not all-powerful. Valentinus probably came closer to the truth with his system of thirty aeons. Thirty may correspond to the number of cosmonauts who invaded the earth twenty thousand years ago. His Demiurge, a name derived from Platonism, conforms to our current notion of their leader. The rest of his thesis, which pictures the demigod and his conquering angels driven frantic when they realize that men's lives were too suddenly invaded by science, is a good approximation of what actually happened."

"And I presume you've been able to reconstruct precisely what happened?" Father Routier inquired with a tinge of sarcasm.

"All we had to do was read and interpret the books

to make the past come alive with luminous clarity. After earth and its climate became organized over a period of some two thousand years, the real task of colonization began, involving a population accustomed to living in caves. Adam probably was among the first to return to the surface, thus serving as a guinea pig for the elohims' experiments consisting of a series of biological procedures based on grafting, selection, and, most important, psychological education. This training of minds was meant to occur gradually and extend over many thousands of years, but Adam and his brethren wanted to forge ahead and acquire knowledge that might have imperiled them in their embryonic stage of evolution. Hence the invaders' anxiety, their efforts to outlaw the forbidden fruit, and, ultimately, their decision to leave earth after first destroying all their installations."

"My dear Moos," the Spirit intervened, "I see now how you visualize the Father: Yahweh, Adonai, Demiurge—a strong leader. But how do you picture the Son? Do you see him as another cosmonaut, one of the elohims who returned to earth some thousands of years after the first invasion?"

"Not at all. I'll get to Christ, whose existence and relative importance I can't deny. It's most unlikely that he was a cosmonaut, since the elohims left without planning to return—of this we have definite proof, but I think it would bore you to hear it. Before leaving, however, they deposited with Noah a scientific legacy

• • • 107 • • •

that permitted man to pursue his development at a reasonable pace. These documents were preserved by priests of the pharaohs; Moses discovered them later buried in the desert sands.

"In the centuries that followed, a succession of sages safeguarded these treasures. Through patient research we have been able to learn their names: after Noah, the Egyptian priests and Moses, came Jesus, who knew the secrets and preached them in the form of good tidings. Thus he founded a civilization that gradually is fulfilling the elohims' prediction, allowing us to 'become like gods,' which simply means as scientific-minded as they were when they developed the means to reach distant planets, a feat we ourselves are about to attempt. Jesus, then, was one of those rare intellects capable of penetrating the truth.

"And that, friends, is all I have to say about your divine power."

V

The cocktail party had gone on longer than most gatherings of this kind. The guests forgot to drink, so eager where they to catch each speaker's every word. The man in the white jacket had retired behind his table and was drowsing, since no one seemed to need his services. It was very late when the last speaker took the floor, the astrophysicist Marcole.

MARCOLE'S DISCOURSE

"Friends, don't expect me to compete with what you've just heard, or you, demon, whose presence is always in my mind, to end your uncertainty. I can't contribute very much to your inquiry because I'm not overly concerned with either the Father or the Son—if indeed they exist, which I doubt."

"I trust," interjected the Holy Spirit, "that I, the Third Person, have some standing in your eyes."

"Your very presence demands my recognition, but if you start interrupting me now, we'll never get through."

"I think it's in your nature and mine to argue; that's part of exchanging ideas. Do go on, though; I'll be quiet and listen."

"I believe in you, dear demon, perhaps more than you do, for I believe in an all-pervading spirit in our universe that affects even its infinitesimal elements and goes undetected by our most advanced instruments. I believe that every atom and every corpuscle constituting the atom possesses that spirit—that is to say, an awareness of its existence comparable to our awareness and just as precise. Thus, every ounce of matter forms a field of self-knowledge, 'sees itself as a whole and in detail,' as Raymond Ruyter has expressed it. So I believe in you, there's no denying it."

"More than I do myself, you're right," grumbled the Spirit, his tone changing. "I never reflected on that point of view before I met you. I still don't understand it fully. But go on; I adore the learning process."

"With regard to the person you call the Father, if you can accept him as the universal consciousness, a consciousness vaster than that of the atom but no less alert, I'd be willing to call him God, though the name has become somewhat sullied. Still, in no way does he resemble the person in your Trinity. A few individuals are just beginning to grasp his true nature."

"Who are these individuals?"

"They are men of science . . . but there's more to it than science. They're a hybrid race. Imagine a cool-headed fanatic or a rational romantic. I think Edgar Allan Poe revealed great understanding of this singular breed when he described with glowing praise the wisdom of a character who was both *poet* and *mathematician*. Such individuals are found among persons who have studied intensely, are still open to astonishment, and can review the results of their arcane calculations with childlike wonder.

"Curiously, dear demon, among these poet-mathematicians one finds almost the same number of specialists working in opposite fields: I mean atomic physicists, whose domain is infinitely small, and astronomers, whose empire is infinity. And it's also remarkable that each has discovered the spirit in his own particular sphere: atomic physicists in corpuscles, astronomers in the nebula, in clusters of nebulae, and in the universe as a whole. Jean Charon discovered this spirit in the electron; Fred Hoyle, contemplating two equations on the heights of Palomar, learned it from a dark cloud the size of a galaxy. Some people might take this as an illustration of professional corruption."

"And aren't you an astrophysicist?"

"Correct. And therefore I'm led quite naturally to believe there is spirit everywhere. 'All things teem with godliness!'"

"These ideas haven't yet reached heaven," murmured the Spirit pensively. "You've opened new worlds for me and I'm grateful to you. . . . But let's come back to the Son. Where does the Son fit into all this, dear Socrates?"

"The Son, dear demon, seems even less important to me than the Father. As Ruyter again observes, the neo-Gnostics point out—correctly, I would say—that 'the simian who stood up on his hind legs played a far greater role in the evolution of life than did Jesus.'"

This statement brought sharp protests from the two churchmen. Marcole calmed them down with a wave of his hand and apologized for airing his own convictions.

"I'm grateful," said Father Routier, somewhat appeased, "that you're not a hopeless atheist and have a certain respect for divinity. But your cosmic consciousness strikes me as an intellectual abstraction as farfetched as all the entities people have tried to substitute for the Almighty. So you've never felt the need for Jesus?"

"You're wrong about that, my friend. I concede that the Son was an element needed ages ago to counteract some of the cruel mistakes humanity made in its representation of divine power. Compared to the Father, whom I keep imagining as a Hitler or a Stalin, he stands for progress, I'll admit—a small step forward on the road to evolution, a well-developed machine for its time..."

"A machine!" Routier expostulated.

"We're all machines. I'll tell you what I really believe—my creed—since everyone here has confessed his own: I'm convinced that most present-day religions are to wisdom what yesterday's alchemy was to science, what astrology was to astronomy, what the musings of Democritus were to atomic theory."

"What a nerve!" Reverend Roberts and Dr. Ahmrad exclaimed in unison.

"Don't get angry. I have the greatest respect for those alchemists, astrologers, and also Democritus.

He had an intuitive vision of reality—true, a rough, imperfect vision in need of being refined, improved, and shorn of irrelevancies, which is what came about in time. Evolution took place in the scientific field, as well as in the industrial one, where it is sometimes called revolution. It has yet to happen in the domain of religion.

"The Father's odious ruthlessness demanded reparation. Jesus provided this betterment, which explains his success. Father Teilhard's universal Christ added a further touch to primitive ingenuity, another improvement and a rather important one in my estimation, for it opens the door to a concept of cosmic consciousness, which seems to be the highest rung on the ladder that we machines can attain for the present, being a little more perfect than our ancestors. I believe further changes will occur, so that from the murky magma of contemporary religions will finally emerge a rational perception of the universe and its soul. . . .

"Friends and demon, there you have my exceedingly modest effort at solving the problems that trouble us all.

"Are you satisfied with this exchange of views?" Marcole asked after the silence that greeted his final words. "No one seems to have anything to add."

"I'm not sure I understand very much more than before," murmured the Spirit. "It will take me a while to absorb what I've heard. Anyway, thank you all for presenting your convictions with such candor."

The night was nearly over. The glasses had been standing empty for hours. Blaming himself for his neglect as host, the astrophysicist woke up the bartender and urged his guests to order one last drink to friendship before the meeting ended. Father Routier and others took champagne, Reverend Roberts had a second whiskey, and Dr. Ahmrad a glass of fruit juice.

Marcole, perhaps after one last inner dialogue with his demon, ordered a cocktail very popular in its day but gone out of fashion since, calling for a mixture of ingredients with varying densities. When the man in the white jacket brought it to him on a platter, he picked up the glass and held it out at arm's length, bowing to each of his guests in turn as if toasting them. He and everyone else stared in fascination at the iridescent rainbow cast by the lamplight on the different levels of liquid.

After completing his bows, he raised his glass higher, as if offering sacrifice to some mysterious divinity. Shaking his head solemnly, he shrugged his shoulders and downed the concoction in a single gulp, as recommended by the drink's inventor.

PART THREE

MARY

I

Mary Queen's popularity had grown steadily since she entered the government. Not only was she remarkably competent, but her outspoken championship of women's rights earned her the overwhelming and undying loyalty of her own sex. This national acclaim, together with a number of astute observations she had made at Cabinet meetings—remarks indicative of a broad perspective reaching far beyond her own special areas of concern—gave President Dumont-Gayol the idea of selecting her for a more important job. It was generally known he had been considering this for some time, and well-informed sources insisted that Mary Queen would be the next prime minister. The chief of state decided to offer her the post in view of her incredibly high rating in the latest polls, for he was convinced that only such a popular figure would be able to push through the unpopular legislation he planned to introduce. Mary's divinity had no bearing on his choice or even crossed his mind.

Touched and flattered by the offer, for form's sake Mary asked to think it over for a few days. She made a point of consulting Mme de Fonteneige and the steering committee of the Association for the Dignity of Women, having agreed to accept the honorary presidency of this organization, provided Mme de Fonteneige continued as acting president. The advice she sought occasionally from the committeewomen had proved useful in formulating some of her official policies. The members all urged her to accept the offer and felt proud of the honor that would thereby reflect on the Association.

As she left the meeting, feeling like a queen, her ears still ringing with adulation, she declined Mme de Fonteneige's invitation to tea and said she needed some time to herself before making a major decision bearing on her future career.

Mme de Fonteneige did not press her. Alone for a change, since she was always dealing with people in her work, Mary looked pensive as she made her way along crowded, noisy streets. It was true that she needed time to reflect. The whirlwind of activity that had swept her up from the moment she arrived scarcely left her time to breathe. Her intense involvement in human affairs, coupled with the desire to succeed at her job and thus merit the trust placed in her, tended to overshadow her commitment to the mission she had undertaken with the Holy Ghost. As a matter of fact, she rarely had a chance to sound out religious attitudes in the circles she frequented. Her cautious questions on the subject had prompted the usual responses and merely confirmed that the Son's image was definitely rising and the Father's waning. Neither Mme de Fonteneige nor her friends at the Association shared her anguish over the mystery of the Trinity. They felt content just to be "religious," which to them meant leaving all decision-making to the Catholic authorities.

After a long walk Mary found herself in front of a church in a strange district. Absorbed in her own thoughts, she hadn't noticed it until she looked up to cross the street. She hesitated, then decided to go in.

The church was nearly deserted. Shyly, she crept along the back pew of the nave and sat down for a moment. Intimidated by the silence, and perhaps by the thought that she had made some blunder, she slipped to her knees, glancing fearfully around her. It was the first time she had entered a church except for attending Sunday mass, which she did regularly, less out of piety than so as not to disappoint Mme de

Fonteneige. At those times she would study intently the expressions of her women companions and try to imagine what they were thinking as they prayed, but that gave her no chance to commune with herself, which she now felt compelled to do.

She couldn't. Her mind focused entirely on the chief of state's offer. The prospect of greater responsibilities and the status attached to the second highest office in the land so thrilled her that she found it impossible to turn her thoughts heavenward.

She chided herself and tried once more to pray, evoking images of paradise. Again she had to give up, uncertain to which supreme deity she should address her prayer: the Father, whom she respected but really feared, or the Son, whom she had once embraced with a mother's love but could never make herself recognize as divine, despite all the theological decrees, and whose overwhelming ambition she deplored.

She hesitated, then decided to visit the chapels bordering the nave. Along one aisle she stopped in front of a primitive painting representing God the Father in glory, enthroned in the clouds among hosts of angels. She stood contemplating the picture, then moved on, shaking her head, feeling no emotion.

She was aware of a slight inner stir as she gazed at the Stations of the Cross and lingered longer, meditating on this series of paintings. The last one caught her attention. It depicted the Virgin at the feet of the crucified Christ. That subject alone brought tears to her eyes.

o   o   o

She dabbed her eyes furtively and continued walking. As she rounded a pillar she came face to face with a priest. It was Father Routier, who lived near the church and came there regularly to pray. She hadn't seen him since the night of the apparition. He recognized her and began to fidget, still unable to decide whether this creature, who haunted his thoughts day and night, came from heaven or the other place. Forcing himself to greet her, he whispered, "I'm glad our paths have crossed in a holy place."

"Yes," Mary replied, "for I have so few opportunities to talk to churchmen. May I ask you a few questions?"

He stared at her aghast, but couldn't run away. "Y-e-s. I'll answer them if I can."

"What do you think of my son Jesus?"

Routier's mental stability tended to desert him when confronted with this woman's unorthodox method of gathering information. Trembling, he replied, "Sister, or Holy Mother, please don't ask me such questions. Remember that we are in his sanctuary."

"Is he really God?" Mary pursued doggedly. "Is he God as he was led to believe by your earthly pronouncements? Or is he a subordinate of the Father?"

"Your persistent inquisition is purposeless—and shocking. He is God. There is no subordination, only equality—I mean identity."

"But if there's identity, he can't be a separate person," Mary objected, stubborn and determined.

"There is both identity and separateness," Routier declared with insistence that merely served to mask his mounting discomfort. "That is the great mystery of the Holy Trinity."

"Mysteries make me nervous," Mary sighed. "For centuries I've been enveloped by mysteries."

Father Routier was moved by the mournful, anguished tone of her voice. "Sister, or Holy Mother," he said, "dismiss those troublesome thoughts and let us pray together. It will surely bring you peace of mind."

Mary knelt beside him. He began to recite the Lord's Prayer. Obediently, she repeated the words after him, stopping only when she came to "Forgive us our trespasses," when she made a polite gesture signifying that this could never apply to her, the Immaculate.

A second prayer followed. She repeated earnestly several times, "Creator of heaven and earth" as if trying to convince herself of it, but when the priest intoned, "... and in Jesus Christ his only son ... seated at the right hand of God," she promptly interjected, "There can be no doubt about it: they are two separate persons, since the Son is seated at the Father's right. That I can see clearly."

"Don't be too sure of it."

"Father, they can't be identical," Mary exulted, obstinate as ever, having developed perseverance in the course of many political debates. "They are *not* one and the same."

"We'll never get through with this," stammered the priest, totally exasperated. "I keep telling you—it's the great mystery."

"Another mystery," Mary sighed wearily, "when I'm so eager to see the light."

She walked away after exchanging a few more comments indicative of her preoccupation. Routier felt relieved to end a conversation that caused him such discomfort and hurried out of the church.

o   o   o

Mary continued down the aisle and came to a chapel brightly lit with scores of votive candles. She went in and felt better at once, as if the air were purer. It was a chapel dedicated to the Virgin. On the walls hung simple paintings of the Madonna, cradling the Christchild in her arms, or prostrate at the foot of the cross, or rising to heaven in her glorious Assumption, surrounded by cherubim. Unlike other parts of the church, this one was not deserted. A number of women were on their knees praying fervently before the holy images. Seeing that this shrine dedicated to her was the only place where the pious chose to gather, Mary felt strangely proud and elated. Her face shone. It was as if she were hypnotized by the candles flickering at various levels, casting a magic glow throughout the chapel and creating shifting patterns of light and shadow on images that almost seemed to come alive.

Impulsively, she fell to her knees beside the other women and found herself praying as ardently as they. She prayed for a long time, and when at last she raised her head, her eyes sparkled with a strange mixture of joy and renewed confidence, as if a long period of mental anguish were ending and she now glimpsed a profoundly thrilling way to solve all her problems.

II

The Holy Spirit felt cheered by Mary Queen's promotion, certain it would assure him greater authority over human souls. He returned to heaven to inform the Father of these developments and of his own progress, which up to now had been minimal and quite discouraging, apart from some intellectual rewards.

He found the Father looking as neglected as ever, still forlorn and resentful. After making his report, the Spirit was bombarded with an avalanche of grievances that soon became tiresome. Feeling depressed by the dreary atmosphere of a palace that reeked of mildew, he offered to go find the Son and make one last attempt to iron out the situation.

"Don't worry, I'm not going to placate him, Lord. You know I'm loyal to you. But I've always had a flair for diplomacy, and one or two concessions on each side might just solve the problem."

"I've made all the concessions I can," sighed the Father, "and what do I get for it but his contempt and the insolent reply he sent me to the effect that I shouldn't have forsaken him when I did. However, if you want to try, I won't stop you. Tell him I'm prepared to offer forgiveness in return for his allegiance. I think I know him pretty well by now; he'll reject any compromise."

So the Holy Spirit went in search of the Son, more curious than hopeful of success. He found him enthroned in luminous glory, attended by rustling choirs of gauzy-winged angels chanting his praises, which he acknowledged with a victor's smile.

The Spirit was struck by the contrast between this excited, enthusiastic host of followers and the thin ranks of dull-eyed old-timers in the Father's court whose monotonous, spiritless mumbling lacked conviction. The Son seemed the very symbol of triumph— an exaggerated triumph, reflected the Spirit, who preferred moderation in all things and was beginning to lose patience at the sight of all this posturing.

The two personalities had dealt politely, if not cordially, with each other in the past. The Son felt slightly envious of the Spirit for having been elevated by theologians to a rank equal to his, yet he knew perfectly well that the Spirit was too blurred an image in people's minds to threaten him as a rival. He also knew that the Spirit was unconcerned by the question of his own divinity and set no store by it. He had long suspected that the Father had sent the Third Person to earth on a mission designed more or less to humble him, but his newly acquired pride made him deride and discount these efforts. The clouds of incense wafting from earth and heaven had convinced him he would soon triumph over the Father and oust him.

In this frame of mind he greeted the Holy Spirit in sarcastic tones overlaid with joviality. "So my brother has returned—after failing in his mission, I do believe?"

Hurt to the quick, the Spirit had all he could do to retain his self-control and reply evenly, "I'm about to return to earth to carry on my task of adjusting the balance of prayers addressed to the Father and to you. The current imbalance strikes me as unhealthy and likely to cause trouble in the world. I might add that I've just talked to the Father and he seems very depressed by the situation. He regrets your departure, which has shattered the harmony in paradise and threatens the celestial hosts with chaos. In brief, the Father will open his arms to you if you will return to him."

"And he offers me a small spot in his shadow?"

• • • 129 • • •

"It's the most honored place in heaven."

"After his own. That's not enough. Tell me, what does one have to do to be welcomed back?"

"Simply pay him homage and acknowledge your loyalty."

"That's all?" sneered the Son. "And repudiate the work of the world's most brilliant theologians over twenty centuries? Simply erase with one swat the decrees of a half-dozen ecumenical councils established by the finest legal talent? Can you hear him, all of you?" he shouted to the crowd of winged courtiers ringing his throne. "He would stick me next to people like Arius, Nestorius, and all the other heretics whom the religious authorities repudiated time after time and excommunicated! What do you think of that? Is that what I deserve—I, a God apart?"

Hearing him say this and deliberately side with the authorities, the Spirit realized the Son had changed a good deal more than he suspected and could never be induced to accept a compromise. The response from his attendants came promptly. Murmurs of indignation followed by a concert of vociferous protests rose from the winged tribe and filled the new throne room. "You can't do that, Lord! You're as good a God as the Father, better than the Father! You're our sole God!" shouted the young angels. "And if you should feel tempted to do it out of excessive humility, we'll stop you and keep you here with us!"

"There you are, my brother," declared the Son. "You have heard them. Even if I wanted to, I couldn't give in. My loyal subjects won't let me desert them. Go tell your master that it's out of the question for me to accept such a humiliation."

"This quarrel threatens to end in civil war," murmured the Spirit, uneasy amid all the agitation.

"Civil war, you say? Impossible," asserted the Son, reverting to the subdued manner he had once favored. "If my cheek is struck, I turn the other one. You know that and so does the Father. So he's defeated before he starts. He can't lift a finger against me."

Resigned, the Spirit didn't bother to point out what appeared to be an absence of logic.

"We would fight!" shouted the angel chorus.

The Son quieted them with a gesture and went on. "I don't have to fight, for I'm already winning. Didn't you hear the words my vicar—you notice that he was never called the Father's vicar—spoke at his enthronement? *Sia laudate Jesu Christo!* May Jesus Christ be praised! The Son, you hear me, the Son, not the Father!"

"Indeed, I hear it all too well," sighed the Spirit.

"May Jesus Christ be praised!" shouted the angelic hosts. "May Jesus Christ be praised!"

These were the very words the Spirit had reported to the Father and that had so infuriated him.

"He continued to pay me tribute, clearly and

openly, during the installation ceremony. The saints and angels who attend me here piously noted his words and keep repeating them to me. Listen: 'O Christ...'"

"O Christ, make me now and forever a servant of your peerless authority."

"Peerless, peerless, do you hear!" the Son announced triumphantly. "And again, 'Brothers and sisters...'"

"Brothers and sisters," intoned the chorus, "be not afraid to welcome Christ and accept his dominion."

"Dominion, dominion!" the Son declared jubilantly. "And then, 'Fling open the gates...'"

"Fling open the gates to Christ and to his redeeming power."

"Power, power! And this: 'Fear not...'"

"Fear not," cried the angels, "fear not, for Christ knows what lies in the hearts of men. And he alone knows."

"He alone, he alone, he alone!" the Son repeated exultantly. "Have you read the encyclical he just published? That's a communication in which every word counts. It begins thus: 'The redeemer of mankind, Jesus Christ, is the center of the cosmos and of history.' The center of the cosmos, do you hear? He goes on to say, 'The sole focus of our spirit, the single direction of our intelligence, our will, and our heart is Christ the redeemer of mankind, Christ redeemer of the world.' Single and sole! The entire document is in the same vein. It's addressed to me and me alone. Do you need to hear more? Did my vicar have anything significant to say to the Father?"

Exasperated, the Spirit cut him short. "That will do. You win for the moment. It's true that the Father's name hardly ever came up during the ceremonies or in your vicar's encyclical. On the other hand..."

"What other hand?"

The Spirit paused. Feeling a sudden urge to squelch this brash upstart whose success was going to his head, he thought he had hit on the best way to do it. With a faint insubstantial smirk, he savored the pleasure he would have in pouring cold water on the conceited fellow. From time to time the Holy Spirit amused himself by teasing people overly impressed by their own self-importance; he enjoyed the sport immensely. "On the other hand, he also spoke of Mary in his first address, and afterward too, in very flattering terms."

"What's that?" snapped the Son, frowning. "I wasn't told about that."

Then the Spirit knew he had struck a sensitive spot and stepped up his sarcastic assault with the retort, "Probably you were too wrapped up in all the adulation you were getting."

"What exactly did he say? Tell me. I want to know."

The Spirit reported with keen pleasure precisely what the pope had said. "He mentioned her several times, my Lord and brother, several times. First he said that he had accepted the office 'in a spirit of obedience to Jesus Christ and trust in the Holy Virgin.' He linked her name with yours, you see."

"Purely out of politeness, no doubt," the Son murmured scornfully.

"No doubt. I should add that the crowds below in the square roared their approval when he uttered the Holy Virgin's name."

"You're not suggesting it was as loud as the first time he mentioned me?" queried the Son, unable to conceal his anxiety.

"At least as loud; it seemed louder, but I can't say for certain. . . . Oh, I almost forgot. Later, he added, 'I come before you to confess our common faith, our hope, our trust in the mother of God.' He wasn't talking about you there, except indirectly."

"Our trust again," exclaimed the Son, visibly alarmed.

"I don't want to bore you by repeating everything he said. Bear in mind simply that he mentioned Mary's name in every address he made, and each time it was roundly applauded. As for the encyclical you quote and seem to know by heart, he may have started out speaking of you, but he ended praising your mother. I was happy for her because up here she never received the recognition she deserved."

He loved to stir up trouble and jealousy in the Second Person, and having done so, departed in excellent spirits. "Poor Mary," he said to himself as he returned to earth, "will she laugh when I tell her about the conversation! Anyway, that pesky young fellow really deserved a lesson."

III

Mary didn't laugh.

When the Holy Spirit told her about his visit, which he found most entertaining, she didn't even smile but took the whole matter very seriously. Her reaction was this: "I noted those statements of the new pope myself along with several other references to me. I'm quite satisfied. Isn't it about time Christendom's leader should render due homage to the mother of God?"

o   o   o

Mary had at least three good reasons to feel satisfied about her visit to earth. The first related to her position as prime minister. Being the central figure in the government (second only to the president, she reminded herself often enough with a sigh of regret) filled her with joy and pride.

Another reason was the devoted nationwide support she continued to enjoy. Her popularity never diminished as a result of her appointment to a thankless job. This loyalty to her person made her even prouder, as she realized it was meant to reward her human virtues, not her celestial status, since very few people knew her real identity. Her prestige extended up and down the social ladder, from President Dumont-Gayol, who thus was able to enact some unpopular measures without too much protest, down to all the ordinary folk. Mary paid close attention these days to her ratings in the polls. She never had to worry, however, for her favor rose steadily and this acted on her like a potent tonic. Her television appearances were enormously successful, and the front-page photographs of her that appeared regularly in the papers did as much to enhance her image as her remarkable skill in handling public affairs. She took care not to neglect her appearance, having learned from the start that this was a major element of her popularity. With the help of Mme de Fonteneige, an expert in such matters, she contrived to improve and embellish her looks. Those big gray eyes became even bigger under a light touch of mascara, and the Greek hairdo she had adopted caused President Dumont-Gayol (who by now had completely forgotten where she came from) to remark, "Minerva! A pagan goddess—that's who she reminds me of. She has the features and the bearing."

The third and not the least source of delight to Mary was the earthly veneration of her heavenly person, the Holy Mother of God. This cult, even if she couldn't boast about it openly, began to seem like her well-deserved reward for having put up so long with the subtly patronizing airs of the saints and angels in paradise. The realization that she had been wronged by having been denied the reins of power made her sorry for herself. Up above, the same three persons went on sharing the limelight, with periods of eclipse for one or another of them—today the Father, yesterday the Son or the Holy Spirit occasioned by some heresy or other—but one of the three always claimed the glorious throne.

So the recognition she was now receiving as a political leader and a woman merged with the prayers offered to her celestial image and made her head reel, as if from clouds of incense and alcoholic vapors.

o　　o　　o

Her reply took the Spirit by surprise, though he didn't show it. He sensed a note of excitement in what she had to say next.

• • • 138 • • •

"Have you seen the latest polls? Seventy-five percent approve Mary Queen's performance in office. A new record. Last time I had established a record at sixty percent."

He was about to congratulate her but didn't get the chance as she pursued her thought with manifest relish. "And did you notice the monogram 'M' on the coat of arms of Christendom's leader? 'M' stands for Mary and nothing else. His veneration of me is apparent in each speech he makes, each action he takes: masses in churches dedicated to the Holy Virgin, and the high mass he will celebrate to mark the centenary of my apparition to Bernadette. He never misses a chance to pay me tribute."

"I noticed that," said the Spirit, finally able to get a word in. "Reverend Roberts and the reformers might be inclined to label it fetishism," he added to himself.

He was aware of a change in Mary's attitude toward him, a series of small things he found it hard to pinpoint but that seemed to herald a new relationship between them. He dismissed an unpleasant thought, telling himself that the prestige and popular regard she seemed to prize so much were important assets in terms of their mission's success. He complimented her for her leadership and the high office she had won, which would enable her to exert a broad influence in behalf of the Father.

Mary smiled and said merely that she would do her best to uphold justice. "For all men, of course, and especially for women, who really need it," she added.

He then asked her if she saw Mme de Fonteneige and the ladies of the Association for the Dignity of Women often.

"Very often," she replied. "They've been a great help to me and have opened my eyes to many things."

The Spirit dropped the subject and began telling her about his recent visit to paradise. He described the forlorn neglect and sadness of the Father in terms designed to arouse her sympathy. She listened absently, a mysterious smile illuminating her Madonna's features from time to time, a smile that may have contained some pity but behind which the Spirit, always quick to discern shades of meaning, detected a hint of scorn. Her attitude changed when he mentioned the Son's ascendancy and his insolent pride. He saw her smile vanish and her clear brow cloud over in a scowl she could scarcely disguise, a scowl that reminded him momentarily of how the ancient bards described the expression on their gods and goddesses. He ended his account with the opinion that it was time to wind up their mission and to instill some degree of humility in the Son.

"I'll do my part," Mary declared, this time with conviction. "I'll do my best. You have my word."

He had to be content with her promise and left her. Thinking back a while later on their conversation, he was finally able to identify the slight difference in

Mary's behavior that had made him uneasy: she had spoken to him as if he were just any ordinary individual. She had not addressed him respectfully as "Lord," which she had never failed to do in heaven in her humbler days. Nor had she called him "my beloved son," a term of endearment she used when she remembered he was God and she therefore his mother. Nor even "my dear and good friend," an instinctive mode of address when her maternal impulse capitulated to a rush of ancient memories.

IV

The friendly understanding between the nation's first and second leaders lasted only a few months, during which Mary submitted reluctantly to the president's authority and executed his instructions without comment. Then their relations grew murky. Successive polls indicating Mary Queen's ballooning popularity began to vex the chief of state, all the more since his own star was fading. As for Mary, little by little the constant stream of praise from press and other media promoted in her a flippant attitude that verged on insolence. At first Dumont-Gayol felt annoyed at her behavior, then seriously alarmed when, as election day approached, there were rumors in political circles that Mary Queen might run for office and would probably win if she did.

She thought about it. Being under the president's thumb was becoming intolerable, and the prospect of climbing to the very pinnacle of power appealed to her as altogether natural and exciting. Mulling over these thoughts one day as she walked alone, she found herself back at the church where she had once tried to pray. She went in, started for a dark corner, and, with her head cupped in her hands, began to reflect on the challenge that lay before her.

"I suppose you are here for confession, my sister. I am at your service."

Without thinking, she had sat down near a confessional from which a woman now emerged. Surprised that the sitter hadn't moved, the priest approached Mary. His question struck her as insulting, if not blasphemous. With an indignant gesture of denial, she snapped, "I didn't come here to make confession."

"Really?" the priest smiled. "Excuse me. Seeing you there, I thought... But are you sure that wasn't your purpose? Sometimes one hesitates at the last moment."

Outraged, Mary responded sharply, "I've no need to make confession."

"Are you certain? Sooner or later all of us, myself included, commit some sin or other that needs forgiveness."

"Not I," Mary corrected him. "I am immaculate in body and soul. I have never committed a sin, not even the original sin. I shall never commit one. That's an article of your faith."

"Not even the sin of pride?" he asked, eying her attentively.

She nearly exploded, a habit she had recently acquired. She was furious with the priest as much for his insulting questions as for his failure to recognize a face that should have been familiar to anyone who read the papers or watched television. Only when she saw that his eyeglasses had very thick lenses did she manage to smother her rage. "Not even that. I tell you that I am spotless, and I don't allow anyone to question it."

"My sister," said the priest after a pause, "if you don't wish to make confession, perhaps you would like to say a prayer with me?"

Father Routier had made the same suggestion once before in this very place. Was it the only word these priests knew? "A prayer to whom?" she exclaimed rebelliously.

"My sister, in your present state of mind," said the priest after a moment's reflection, "I urge you to pray to the very symbol of humility and saintly virtue, the Virgin."

"I'm willing to try," Mary conceded, relaxing a bit.

The priest knelt and began, "Hail Mary, full of grace."

"Hail Mary, full of grace," she recited with unwonted conviction.

The priest continued until he came to the phrase, "Holy Mary, mother of God."

"Mother of God, mother of God," she stressed each syllable, repeating the words over and over fervently as if gripped by a sudden revelation.

"Then is she really the mother of God?" Mary asked as the priest crossed himself and rose to his feet.

"We may not doubt that it is so."

"Which means not only the mother of Christ and mother of the Holy Spirit, but mother of the Father as well, since all three are one single God. . . . Thank you very much," Mary concluded in a ringing voice. "You have helped me to cast out the darkness."

Tired of this conversation, the priest exhorted her to humble herself before the Almighty and left, as a radiant smile crept across Mary's face.

Alone now, she made her way to the front of the church, walking with firm and confident steps. She didn't even glance at the painting of the Father enthroned among the angels. She didn't stop before the different stations of the cross. As if drawn by a magnet, she headed straight for the chapel sacred to the Virgin. She had thought of it often since her first visit, returning to contemplate it for hours in her imagination, it so fascinated her.

Her hopes were not deceived. She stopped at the entrance, delighted to discover the shrine filled with worshipers. It was the month dedicated to the Virgin; every day the little chapel was filled with women at prayer.

"It's the month of Mary," the candle vendor whispered to her. "Oh! It's the prime minister! It's Mary Queen!" And having recognized her, the woman dropped to her knees. Mary smiled and placed a finger over her lips, indicating that she didn't want her presence known to the women at prayer, who were too absorbed in their devotions to notice her.

Mary knelt behind the last row of seats, hid her face in her hands, and joined the chorus of voices, repeating rapturously over and over (which caused some heads to turn around), "Mother of God! Mother of God!" These simple words suddenly had taken on a new and miraculous significance for her.

V

Leaving the women to their prayers and canticles, Mary stole out of the chapel, unrecognized except by the woman selling votive candles, who insisted on walking her to the church entrance with a great show of deference.

Just in front of the inner door of the vestibule sat a poor cripple with both legs paralyzed, who appeared on certain days in his battered wheelchair to beg for his living. When Mary, followed by the candle seller, walked past the man, he stretched out his hand imploringly and barred her way. The candle vendor was about to step between them.

"Let him alone," said Mary. "I belong to everyone, especially to those who suffer."

She reached into her purse for a coin, but her thoughts lay elsewhere. She stared intently at the man's useless limbs, while he in turn appeared fascinated by her scrutiny. He dropped his eyes and his outstretched hand, which Mary promptly grabbed. She remained thus for a moment, silent, immobile, engaged in an intense inner struggle, then made a sudden decision. "Get up and walk," she commanded.

Trembling from head to toe, the paralytic stared at her in panic. Mary released his hand and ran her fingers gently over his crippled legs, repeating in a compelling voice tinged with impatience, "Get up and walk."

Then the miracle happened. The touch of that hand, hot as a flame to him, acted on the cripple like an electric shock. He stopped trembling and stared into Mary's eyes as if drawn by their magnetic gleam and her imperious voice. He raised himself out of his wheelchair, pushing himself up first with his arms, then stood on his own two feet, tottered forward a few inches, and finally began to walk more steadily with each step, as the good woman who witnessed this miraculous event fell to her knees.

The beggar turned around and came back to kneel beside her and the two shed tears of joy on the hem of Mary's dress. Mary's face broke into a glow of triumph.

The man raised his eyes shyly toward the miracle-maker and managed to stutter between sobs, "Who are you, you who have healed me? What holy name shall I utter day and night in my prayers until the hour of my death?"

Mary leaned over and kissed his forehead as she whispered, "I am she who is."

"The Holy Virgin!" exclaimed the woman with the candles, as if suddenly inspired. "Holy, Holy Mary, mother of God!"

"Holy Mary, mother of God," the beggar repeated, his face touching the floor.

Before she turned to leave, wearing her most celestial smile, Mary replied, "You have said it."

o   o   o

"Holy Mary, mother of God!" cried a chorus of ladies in the Association for the Dignity of Women, out-voiced by the triumphant soprano of Mme de Fonteneige as she entered the drawing room where the committee was about to meet.

The miraculous curing of the paralytic certainly had not gone unnoticed. The woman with the candles had spread the news and so had the rehabilitated cripple. Viewed skeptically by some, taken seriously by others, the event focused the public eye once again on Mary Queen. In any case, the Association's membership actively supported the idea of a miracle. With Mary's approval, Mme de Fonteneige revealed to the steering committee the real identity of their honorary president and the circumstances of her apparition on earth. The only thing she didn't tell them, for fear that it might cause a scandal, was the object of Mary's mission. Certain members—the baroness, for one— might challenge her story, but along came the miracle of the cured paralytic just in time to prop it up. If some of the ladies still had doubts, they wouldn't admit it. For the honor of the Association, skeptics felt compelled to join hands with absolute believers.

Stunning confirmation of her supernatural powers, which further enhanced her self-image, this miracle left Mary resolved to seek the highest rung on the political ladder. To accept second place was to accept failure, she now felt. As always, however, before making a major decision she wanted to sound out the committeewomen who had supported her so loyally during her rise to fame, particularly Mme de Fonteneige, her acknowledged adviser. This was the purpose of today's meeting.

More dignified than ever, she thanked the ladies for their welcome. Wasting no time, she explained her current situation and the chief of state's attitude toward her. "It began with minor disagreements on minor matters. I made a point of speaking and acting in conformity with the policies he wished me to follow."

"Mother of God!" exclaimed Mme de Fonteneige. She had adopted that mode of address knowing Mary preferred it. "Mother of God, forgive me, but it showed too much condescension on your part."

"Mother of God, she is right," the committee members agreed, "it was up to you to impose your wishes and not to bow to his."

"I wanted to show moderation, but that's becoming ever so difficult. We disagree all the time. Now we argue over what to me are very significant matters. I don't see how I can continue much longer to give in to him."

"It can't be done," declared Mme de Fonteneige. "Keeping you under his thumb that way is more than scandalous, it's sacrilegious. I'll have a word with Dumont-Gayol and remind him of his obligations to you. He used to listen to me."

"It won't do any good. He's stubborn. I thought of another answer: What if I entered the race for president? I believe I have a good chance of winning. First, however, I'd have to resign as prime minister, and do it right away because election time is almost here."

"Mother of God," the baroness nodded approvingly, "you have hit on the best possible answer. I'm certain you will be elected. The country would not dare insult you."

"Still, I wasn't sure and wanted all of you to tell me what you think," said Mary, glancing over the group before her. "If I undertake this project, I will need your approval and backing, not just through prayers, but..."

"Holy Mary, mother of God," came a spontaneous chorus of voices, "Holy Mary, mother of God, you are blessed among women and you may rely on the prayers and the unstinting support of the Association for the Dignity of Women now and forever until the hour of our death. Amen."

"I expected no less of you. Thank you. It's decided, then. Tomorrow I'll turn in my resignation to the chief of state and then devote myself to my election campaign."

With a sign resembling a blessing, Mary drew the meeting to a close. The committeewomen genuflected their way out of the room.

When she was alone with Mary, Mme de Fonteneige told her, "Mother of God, I can't forgive Dumont-Gayol for treating you this way. He is now my enemy. Your election is a sure thing and I'm delighted for you. Still, I'll do everything I can to counteract the effects of his campaign."

"Thank you," Mary replied dreamily. "It promises to be a hard struggle. He is shrewd, eloquent at times, and as incumbent, he possesses more weapons than I despite my popularity. I know he is planning an important press conference to kick off his campaign and intends to announce certain improvements in the economy—most of which are my doing—and claim credit for them. Of course, he will also make grandiose campaign promises."

"I don't see how we can stop him from holding that conference," said Mme de Fonteneige.

"No," Mary said pensively, "but I wonder if it wouldn't be possible to steer it slightly off course. That's where the Holy Spirit could be of great help. His weapons are different from ours and I need every advantage I can muster. I'll ask him to lend a hand. He can't refuse me."

VI

The variety of opinions expressed at the cocktail party had provided little information to the Holy Spirit except that humanity shared no single concept of God. It also had served to reinforce his uncertainty about the nature of the Father and the Son, uncertainty that in time tended to go hand and hand with mounting indifference. Often he was tempted to consider the problem incidental, to forget his mission and spend less time and thought on heavenly affairs than on his conversations with the astrophysicist Marcole, whose person he regularly inhabited in order to learn by asking questions and listening to answers.

In this way he became familiar with the special problems that consumed Marcole. He went with him to a number of scientific meetings and became as excited as everyone else about theories he had never known about in paradise. Because of his exceptional intellectual gifts, he quickly mastered theories of the relativity of time and space, the expanding universe, the big bang, and the concept of continuous creation. He dreamed about the substance of quasars, pulsars, black holes, and all the favorite preoccupations of Marcole that, by a kind of osmosis, began to exert a singular hold over the Third Person.

It took Mary to bring him down to earth again, so to speak, by reminding him of the grave problems in paradise and by asking for his help in the coming election, now that she was an official candidate. "As president, I would be in the best possible position to exercise a decisive influence on human beings," she assured him.

Feeling a little guilty about his past neglect, and despite the fact that his recent conversations with her had planted some doubt in his mind as to her loyalty to the Father, the Holy Spirit resolved to ignore his suspicions and promised to do what he could to help her win. Having thought about it, he decided the best approach would be to needle her principal rival, the outgoing president. Thus he prepared to attend the press conference that Dumont-Gayol had scheduled a few weeks before election day to bolster his prestige and attract voters away from the radiant, mesmerizing image of Mary Queen.

o   o   o

The president had prepared himself thoroughly for the delicate task he performed periodically and that now assumed crucial importance. His staff of experts had been working around the clock for weeks to plan the conference, a ceremony with its own ritual. One set of imaginative minds had the job of anticipating the trickiest questions that might crop up, while a second group worked out all the right answers. A third brainy crew developed themes the president was anxious to promote, while their colleagues devised suitable transitions providing verbal short cuts to those themes via wholly irrelevant questions. One last team collected an arsenal of droll sayings, witty retorts, and scintillating quips designed to evoke approving smiles and sympathetic laughter.

No detail had been overlooked, Dumont-Gayol felt certain, as he supervised all these activities, having first laid out guidelines. He predicted that his careful, thorough handling of every topic would demonstrate his political superiority over Mary Queen, whose defiance he could not forgive after everything he had done for her.

As he stepped before the cameras in the room packed with hundreds of newsmen he was in excellent spirits. The conference began just as he had planned. His replies to the first few questions drew favorable murmurs; his witty observations provoked flattering smiles. He felt confident he was winning the encounter and waited impatiently for the question that would launch him on those two painstakingly prepared lines that were the heart of his message. He smiled benignly as the reporter from *The Clarion* rose and asked to speak. A long-time ally of the establishment, *The Clarion* would never set out to trap him. In any case, Dumont-Gayol had been informed that the question would be one of those designed to shunt him, via a smooth and natural transition, onto his major theme. The reporter conducted himself with the dignity and propriety characteristic of all that newspaper's representatives and that set them apart from other journalists.

"Lebois, Mr. President, from *The Clarion*."

The president's eyelids fluttered in surprise. He knew the reporter, having talked to him several times, and felt there was something oddly unfamiliar about the man's voice. It was indeed Lebois speaking, dignified and respectful as ever, but with a slightly authoritative note that vaguely reminded Dumont-Gayol of another voice he had heard before but couldn't quite place. This note of authority was also perceived by most of the president's staff, who sensed that something unforeseen was about to happen and held their breath. Not the least flustered, the chief of state spoke with an engaging smile. "Ask your question."

"Here it is, Mr. President," the Holy Spirit began. ... He had borrowed the person of Lebois on advice from Marcole, who felt that a reporter from *The Clarion* would be more receptive than anyone else to various influences. And in fact he had met no resistance. "Mr. President, I should like to know your opinion on expansion."

That wasn't the question they had planned. Dumont-Gayol's staff pricked up their ears and began to feel alarmed.

"I believe I've already covered that subject," said the president, mildly disconcerted. "Weren't you listening? I'll say it again if you like. Briefly, I favor a moderate but constant expansion."

"Excuse me, Mr. President, but that isn't what I meant. I was talking about the expansion of the universe. I'll explain, if you don't mind. The expanding universe is a fact recognized today by the majority of scientists, though they disagree radically as to the outcome of that expansion. Some feel it will continue forever and end in an infinite dilution. Others speculate that it may gradually slow down, reach its maximum, and then contract and return to its original state. Many others won't even hazard a guess, as they feel that either supposition is a definite possibility. *The Clarion*'s readers and I are anxious to know more about this issue and would welcome your opinion, Mr. President."

Muffled snickers broke out all over the room. Eyes were riveted on Dumont-Gayol as everyone strained to observe his reaction to a question suggesting either that the deferential Lebois had indulged a sudden urge to impudence or else had simply gone beserk, though neither alternative sounded characteristic of a reporter for *The Clarion*.

Then something quite strange and unexpected happened. The president didn't flash one of his indulgent smiles that forgave and sometimes dismissed unseemly queries. Nor did he get angry; if one eyebrow remained cocked, anger was not the cause of it. He appeared lost in dreamy meditation, as if the newsman's question had loosed a chain of unfamiliar thoughts. It was his turn to be haunted by the Spirit. He was unaware of the sea of faces surrounding him. He had completely forgotten the lessons painstakingly memorized in the weeks before and no longer thought of shunting an unfriendly question onto friendlier tracks, an art he had mastered. He was absorbed by the problem presented to him, which called to mind an article in a popular science magazine he had skimmed through a while back and put aside, engrossed as always in his official duties.

After a few moments he seemed to come out of his daydream, still under the Spirit's sway, and replied with the same solemnity as his interlocutor. "It's a matter that requires lengthy investigation and testing as well as careful sifting of the facts and current theories. I can't give you an answer now, M. Lebois, but I promise that a study will be made."

"Thank you, Mr. President," stammered Lebois, who had regained his own personality and was casting frantic glances around the room.

His poise returned. The stir caused by his intervention and the president's reaction gradually died down. Another newsman stood up and asked the anticipated question dealing with an area of foreign policy calculated to show Dumont-Gayol at his best, with all the answers at his fingertips.

The president's performance was listless. His staff, after laboring for nights on end to prepare his replies, despaired as they saw him hesitate and heard him fumbling for words devoid of conviction, as if he were obsessed by something totally unrelated to his subject. Nerves reached a pitch, and someone called it scandalous when the president stopped abruptly in the middle of a sentence and shouted "Eureka!", his face aglow with pleasure. Glancing over to the row in which Lebois was sitting, he announced triumphantly, "Now, about the problem that is bothering you, M. Lebois, and that also is on my mind, believe me—the future of the universe—I can at least confirm that either of the two postulates you cite is feasible; the truth depends on the density of matter in the universe."

With the Spirit stimulating his excellent memory,

he was able to recall the conclusion of the article he had read hastily a month before. His self-satisfaction took an unexpected detour as he added, "May I inquire, M. Lebois, what prompted you to ask me such a question?"

Possessing in turn the reporter and the chief of state, the Spirit replied, "I was stunned a few days ago when I read a particular sentence in a book that's just been published."

"What did it say?"

"It said, *The conscious effort to understand the universe is one of the rare things that lifts the human soul above the level of farce.*[1]"

"... One of the rare things that lifts the human soul above the level of farce... above the level of farce," Dumont-Gayol repeated pensively. "Excellent."

A reproving silence greeted these words. The Spirit was pleased with the success of his tactics— another suggestion of Marcole's, who felt that the best way to needle the head of government and make him forget his day-to-day concerns was to confront him with a far weightier topic. As far as the astrophysicist was concerned, no subject took precedence over the future of the universe. His strategem was working well, for the president continued speaking.

"Excellent question, sir, and a remarkable quo-

[1] Steven Weinberg, *The First Three Minutes: A Modern View of the Origin of the Universe,* 1976.

tation. I'll give it some thought and hope to provide you with a more detailed reply at our next conference. ... This one is ended, gentlemen," he added. "I believe the main problems have been identified, even if we haven't yet succeeded in resolving them."

Confused and shocked, the staff members watched him get up hastily and disappear out the rear door without his papers or any apology.

He rushed to the private office where he usually closeted himself when deciding major issues of state. Asking his secretary to come in, he told him to lay hands immediately on everything that had been published in the last century on mathematics, physics, astronomy, and cosmology. Alone after catching his breath, and badgered by the Spirit, he reassembled the bits and pieces of his adolescent science courses, taken in the days before he had decided on a political career. With visible pleasure and feverish headwork he began scribbling mysterious equations on a subject he suddenly discovered to be of capital importance.

"... One of the rare things that lifts the human soul above the level of farce, above the level of farce," he kept repeating with a smile during the brief pauses he allowed himself in these scientific cogitations.

VII

"Elected!"

Mary's pale face lit up for an instant, flushed with pride, when, midway through the night, the final election results proclaimed her the people's choice for president—by a majority Mme de Fonteneige alternately described as overwhelming or lavish.

Actually, it came as no surprise. For several weeks the polls had favored her by ever-increasing margins as the deadline neared. Nobody had been willing to wager a penny on the incumbent president after his disastrous press conference with its scandalous conclusion. His own staff found his behavior mystifying and alarming, if not indicative of some incipient mental disorder.

His moods had a strange way of shifting abruptly, almost as if there were two individuals inside him. Sometimes he totally ignored his election campaign and public affairs in general, shutting himself up in his study to pour over his scientific speculations. At other times, when the Spirit had left him and he was his own anguished self, deploring the hours he had wasted over what then appeared to be idiotic pursuits, he would weep bitter tears as the polls told him of his waning prestige and vow to get down to work seriously. This lasted only a short while. The Spirit would return to haunt him, inspiring a burning desire to discover the hidden mechanisms of the universe—an insatiable curiosity the Spirit had acquired from his association with Marcole.

"Elected!"

Mary's exclamation was taken up by a chorus of committeewomen from the Association, her court of honor, and the word became sacred on their lips. Overcome with emotion, Mme de Fonteneige alone dared to embrace the victor. The others dropped to one knee and intoned an improvised prayer.

"Holy Mary, mother of God, at last you are elevated above all women to a position worthy of you. The people have perceived that none but the highest office is good enough for you. Every woman across the land, without exception, has voted for you. They will be rewarded. We all await the boundless benefactions of your rule. May your blessings fall on us throughout your reign, which begins today. May it last seven times seven years, over and over, eternally."

"Thank you," said Mary, smiling through tears that flowed like pearls down her cheeks, "but it's impossible for me to make such pledges, for I belong not just to the world."

"Alas, we understand, beloved mother, but stay with us as long as you can."

"I promise," said Mary. "Meanwhile, I bless you and will do everything in my power for you while I am among you."

After drying her tears and enjoying the first thrill of victory, she meditated quietly for a long time while her sisters kept silent. At last she murmured barely above a whisper, "Yes, everything in my power while I am here. Yet this power is still very limited."

It was no time to indulge in melancholy. The hint of a frown on her forehead vanished as she prepared for her victory celebration. Officials and newsmen poured in and the festivities went on late into the night, interrupted by a lengthy television appearance in which Mary Queen, looking radiant and dignified, proved more than equal to the occasion.

o   o   o

The night was nearly over. She left to get a few hours' rest before tackling her new job. Mme de Fonteneige, who had accompanied her, suddenly announced, "I congratulate you too, dear mother, and bring you compliments and best wishes from paradise, beside the earthly ones."

Mary looked at her blandly. She recognized the peculiar accents of the Holy Spirit when he possessed a human being. "Thank you," she said simply, "but is it worth the trouble in the long run?"

The Spirit gazed at her through Mme de Fonteneige's eyes, amazed at her lack of exuberance. "Of course it's worth the trouble."

Mary shrugged her shoulders and didn't answer.

"Mother dearest, you now hold a key position. You will be able to exercise your influence freely all over the country and help me instill a grain of common sense in these good people. The Father is counting on you to end the great Western schism, as he calls it, and to restore the reverence he deserves. He applauds your election and told me to tell you so."

"The Father, the Father," Mary muttered disdainfully.

"But dearest mother..."

Mary flew into one of those sudden rages that contorted her features. "If I am your dearest mother," she shouted, "is it your place to give me orders? Aren't children supposed to obey their parents? That commandment was set down by the one even you call Father and who also is none other than my son. Am I not the mother of God?"

"You are, you are indeed, mother of God," the Spirit conceded hastily, as much to avoid offending her as because, perhaps owing to his newly acquired scientific instruction, he saw no rational objection to her logic. "You are, and I don't presume to tell you what to do. But aren't we both working for the same goal: to restore peace and harmony to heaven?"

"Harmony to heaven," Mary repeated, serene now and pensive, "that *is* our common goal. I think of it every day and will work for it, have no fear."

"I'm confident that you will, beloved mother."

"I've done a lot of thinking since I came to earth. My view has broadened and become more realistic than it was in my humble station in paradise. As prime minister I handled delicate and urgent matters, always successfully—everyone will tell you so, and today's election proves it. . . . And you," she added, looking Mme de Fonteneige squarely in the eyes, "haven't you changed since you began mingling with human-kind?"

"Of course I've learned a good deal more than I could ever guess, and I'm still learning. I've probably changed . . . but not in the same way you have, I suspect," he muttered to himself.

Mary thought a moment, then continued. "Our

· · · 167 · · ·

goal hasn't changed, and it so happens that I think I've discovered the best way to reconcile the Father and the Son."

The Spirit asked her to explain what she meant. A trifle haughtily, she replied, "I'll let you know in good time."

Mary cloaked herself in a brooding silence, then suddenly announced, "Leave me alone. I have a duty to perform before I return home." And off she rushed.

The Spirit abandoned Mme de Fonteneige and left her throbbing with excitement on the street corner while he, perplexed, set out to locate some new and receptive human hosts.

o   o   o

Alone with her thoughts, Mary made her way to the same church she had visited several times before. It was daybreak when she arrived. A few old women sat in the front rows of the nave as the priest celebrated early Mass.

Ignoring the service, she headed briskly for the chapel of the Virgin, making no effort to muffle her footsteps as she traversed the nave with bold, defiant strides. When the priest and his flock turned to glare at her, she gave an angry shrug of her shoulders, meant as much for the ceremony in progress as for the painting of the Father Eternal, her heels hammering contemptuously as she passed.

At the entrance to the chapel she stopped. It was

dark and deserted. Such neglect, even at that early hour, struck her as intolerable and she grimaced from wounded vanity.

No one was selling candles, but she knew where they were kept and the closet door yielded to her furious tugging. She groped inside her purse and drew out several bills that she crumpled and tossed on the ground. Then she proceeded to drag out all the boxes of candles, big ones and small ones alike, which she lit and placed in holders surrounding images of the Madonna. When she ran out of holders she simply set them on the ground in pools of liquified wax.

Gradually the chapel emerged from the darkness and its splendor eclipsed the rest of the church. Paying no heed to the priest and three kneeling women who had stopped praying to stare at her in dismay, she prostrated herself before the images of the Virgin and repeatedly kissed the ground.

VIII

The Holy Spirit had returned to report to the Father, a duty he now considered a chore and had neglected for some time. He found paradise seething with excitement unrelated to the rivalry between the two persons, which had faded into the background as far as the celestial hosts were concerned.

Before reaching the upper regions of heaven, he traveled through various spheres where, to his surprise, he encountered a great commotion. An avalanche of questions descended on him from the saints and lesser angels, delaying his passage to the supreme throne.

"Elected! Elected! Elected!" the tiniest angels rustled, clapping their gauzy, insectlike wings. "Tell us, Holy Spirit, tell us all about this great victory. Only the faintest waves have reached us across the ether, but they were enough to make us all excited."

In fact, nearly a year had passed since the presidential election, but in paradise a year is like one second and the heavenly hosts were celebrating the event as if it had just occurred.

The Holy Spirit met all inquiries with the same, ultimately monotonous, message. "It was only the election of a president in one territory on the planet Earth, and all citizens over the age of eighteen took part. There was no runoff; she won eighty percent of the vote."

"Why only eighty?" demanded some of the elect. "Mary, mother of God and mother of us all, deserved more than that."

But this slight objection was soon forgotten amid the cheers and applause of a group of seraphim who had hurried down from the heavenly heights to mix with the ordinary hosts and who, with their three sets of wings and herculean lungs, managed to produce as much noise as the throng of lesser angels. "Risen in one sublime bound to the highest throne! Alleluia! Alleluia!" they roared. "Long live our mother!"

"Long live our mother!" echoed the cherubim, who had also deserted the palace to come greet the messenger. "Planet Earth has crowned her empress. The whole world has so acknowledged her."

"The universe has seen her excellence and her glory and stands solidly behind her," bellowed the thrones, the virtues, the dominations, and finally the ordinary angels, who were shouting themselves hoarse to spread the good news through space. "Long live the mother of God!"

Escorted and deafened by this jubilant throng, the Holy Spirit came before the Father, as morose as ever and completely out of touch with the outside world in his all but deserted palace. "Lord," said the Spirit after the usual greetings had been exchanged and the tumult subsided, "I'm obliged to admit total failure. Failure, first, among those who practice religion. For the ordinary folk as well as churchmen, in the humblest dwellings as well as in the synods, the Son prevails. And when he is not the focus of attention, the Trinity is."

"Same old hateful Western schism," muttered the Father.

"They're intractable, Lord, and I give up trying to persuade them. It makes more sense to admit that Western man is not yet mature enough for monotheism—neither is Eastern man, for that matter. Each time a few bold heads attempt to establish a single deity, rejection follows, conveyed by the creation of idols that dilute and share his authority and can assume any number of forms."

"Like the Son," the Father grumbled testily.

"Failure also with the little group of scientists I told you about. They're generally taken for atheists, but they strike me as more inclined than are religious people to recognize a single divinity, and I expected to find them fruitful ground for sowing the good word. I soon realized that their cosmic consciousness (that's what they call their deity) had so little in common with you, Lord, that you'd have to change considerably to win their approval."

"Change!" the Father groaned. "My very soul rebels at the word."

"That's the problem, Lord."

"I hope you're sorry," said the Father suspiciously, because the Spirit's voice was not exactly heavy with despair.

"Yes, of course," replied the Spirit indifferently after a pause. . . . "Anyway, these scientists are only a tiny minority. For the bulk of the population, the Western schism is not about to go away. Unless..."

"Unless what?" said the Father hopefully.

The Holy Spirit thought for a moment and replied, "It seemed to me—now, this is only a hasty impression, for I must admit that my own work kept me pretty much to myself these last few months—but it seemed to me that the cult of the Son was showing signs of wear."

"Really?"

"Don't rejoice yet, Lord, for if my impression is correct, this rift will only give way to another. A new idolatry is in the making. Mary..."

"Mary!" cried the Father. "I was relying on her after what you told me about her new position. How is she using the worldly power she holds?"

The Holy Spirit was about to reply and explain what he suspected, based on his latest conversations with Mary, when a thunderous roar shook the heavens, making the palace walls tremble and the glorious throne quiver. Above the peals of acclamation and the blaring trumpets rose a great cry, a single cry from the lips of the celestial multitudes, "She's coming!"

IX

An unusual event, not the sort that appears on the front page of newspapers and on magazine covers all over the world, had occurred on earth.

It happened nearly a year after Mary's election victory. She knew she had worked hard in the public interest, having reorganized the administration to make it more efficient and responsive to her constituents, male and female alike. The impact of her leadership was felt in every area and in every branch of government, where she had installed a number of ladies from the Association for the Dignity of Women. Mme de

Fonteneige had declined an appointment, preferring her role of backstairs adviser, a function she adored and at which she excelled.

It was the first of May. To celebrate this May Day, Mary Queen had organized a mammoth demonstration. The significance of the holiday had been changed by presidential decree from a day honoring labor to the first day in the month of Mary. The fact that this shift in symbols had been accepted without a murmur attested to the nation's veneration of its chief of state. In fact, after the miraculous curing of the paralytic, plus two other equally spectacular performances, and after the account of her apparition spread by the Association's ladies, people were convinced she was a supernatural being and were ready to worship her. Most Frenchmen felt proud and gratified to have been chosen for such a signal honor. Even skeptics and atheists felt that that honor reflected on the whole nation and so kept silent about their doubts. Many foreigners envied the privileged French.

As the site of this public demonstration, Mary had selected a vast plain on the outskirts of the capital. The apotheosis she was secretly planning for the climax of the ceremony called for enormous crowds, not just a little group of devoted worshipers whose testimony could be impugned later on. For this very reason all the television networks had been summoned.

So on this first of May, Mary stepped out on the

platform where government officials and a few guests, mostly women, had already taken their places. Among them, sitting as a group apart, were twelve ladies from the Association, including of course the very visible Mme de Fonteneige, whom Mary had chosen as her most devoted worshipers. She told them her plan before the ceremony started and had given them secret instructions. Their tense faces conveyed a mixture of excitement, disappointment, and hope.

Mary's appearance triggered a standing ovation that reverberated through the countryside for several minutes, during which she stood with one arm raised above her head, making the victory sign with two fingers.

The crowd somehow sensed it would be treated to an extraordinary event just by the fact that Mary wasn't wearing the kind of outfit she usually wore for formal public appearances. She had on the same clothes that thousands of paintings of her had popularized: a floor-length blue gown and a veil framing her face. She had originally planned to put on the same garment she had worn in heaven for two thousand years, the one she wore the night of her materialization in Mme de Fonteneige's drawing room, and which her mentor had piously preserved. After the two friends discussed the matter, she went along with the idea of having a copy made by a famous fashion designer, who kept the general lines of the dress while adding his own artistic flourish to pictorialized mythology. By careful attention to minute details of cut and by choosing a lustrous blue, he succeeded in turning out a dress worthy of a queen. At Mary's request, it was cut low to set off the ribbon of the Legion of Honor she wore across her breast, insignia of her worldly glory that she never would have done without on this occasion.

With a gesture she called for silence; slowly the applause subsided. Then, instead of the traditional playing of the national anthem, hundreds of loudspeakers dotting the plain trumpeted Schubert's "Ave Maria," sung by a Corsican tenor whose muffled accents seemed to impart a celestial resonance to the prayer. Mary listened to the music with the same serene contemplation as her audience, and together they communed in an intensely religious experience. A fresh burst of cheers greeted the final chords. At last she could make the speech she had prepared.

"Women... and men..." Clearly she was addressing the whole world and was not speaking merely as the leader of a single modest-sized country. And her pause between the two sexes, followed by the lowering of her voice after the pause, indicated her high regard for her female audience. "I wish to thank all of you who elected me to the highest office of this land. I hope I will prove worthy of your trust. But today I am obliged to hand over this position to someone else, for it seems that I must occupy another office, an office that has awaited me eternally and that I have neglected too long. It was to announce this decision that I asked you to come here today."

These words set off an uproar and shouts of protest. "Don't leave us, beloved mother! Stay with us!"

"I can't," Mary replied with a smile, adding, "for my kingdom is not of this world."

When it was quiet again, she continued. "Some of you women—and men—know who I am. Others suspect it. Still others question it. I wish to make a formal announcement and to furnish evidence shortly that will vanquish any doubt: I am Mary, mother of God."

She stilled the rising clamor and went on speaking. "But I have other good news of equal importance to reveal to you today, a truth that seems to have escaped the notice of even my most fervent admirers, obvious as it is: Mary, as mother of God, ranks above him in time and space. It is she who possesses the many virtues that too many of you ascribe to other persons who are mere creatures of hers. Eternity is hers. Omnipotence is hers. Infinite bounty is hers and hers alone when she chooses to show compassion. Hers and hers alone is the power to judge the quick and the dead. Have I made myself clear?"

The shrieks and sobs that greeted this declaration demonstrated that the crowd had indeed understood and was prepared to acknowledge her with wild enthusiasm. The interruption lasted several minutes, after which Mary continued.

"To avoid confusion, since the name of God has been sullied too often, I propose to take the title of Goddess, with a capital "G" if you please. You may address me therefore as the Goddess Mary from this day forth. Repeat with me: there is only one Goddess, Mary, who reigns on high. Hers alone is the glory, the sovereign majesty."

"There is only one Goddess," the Association ladies repeated in unison, echoed by all the people. "Hers alone is the glory, the sovereign majesty."

"Before leaving you," Mary went on, "I wish to dictate my law. You will worship no other goddess or god than me. This is my absolute will, my first commandment. For the rest, you may follow the rules that were given you before. If I decide to change them I'll let you know. You may also continue to love your neighbor, as the Son recommended when he was not so full of ambition.

"One last word: I will not forget you. I mingled with the women of this country just as my son walked among the men of Judea. I have done my apprenticeship of authority among you and it has served me well, if only to help me understand myself. I want to thank you women of France, and the men too, for welcoming and recognizing me. You will be my special people, and *for this cause I raised you up, to show in you my power, and that my name may be glorified throughout all the earth.*[1] *Fear not, for even if I shall visit the iniquity of the fathers upon the children unto the third and fourth generation of them that hate me,*[2] *I also show mercy unto thousands of them that love me and keep my commandments.*[2]

"These are my last words on earth. Fall on your knees. Let those with ears listen and let your prayers accompany me to heaven, where I shall now betake myself."

She stretched out her arm to bless the crowd, which had dropped to its knees. After kissing the ground, her worshipers raised their heads, only to find the Goddess floating skyward to the strains of "Ave Maria" blaring once more through the loudspeakers, while the angelic choirs that seemed to spring out of the clouds added their celestial cadences to those of the tenor.

Thousands of ecstatic faces thus witnessed Mary's second Assumption, more glorious and far more spectacular than the first. As her luminous form, flooded with sunlight, melted into the blue sky and the final notes of the Schubert died away, the kneeling crowd began to murmur in unison a new, passionate prayer that opened thus: "Our Mother who reigns in heaven,

[1]*Exodus*, IX, 16
[2]*Deuteronomy*, V, 9–10

thy kingdom come, thy will be done..." while Mme
de Fonteneige and the eleven other disciples dried
their tears and prepared to roam the earth preaching
the new religion.

X

"She's coming!" roared the seraphim, beating the ether furiously with their six shining wings.

"She's coming!" yelled the cherubim.

"She's coming!" shouted the other winged creatures, trying to make as much noise as their archangel superiors. "Our beloved mother returns laden with worldly honors, a new crown upon her brow. Glory, glory to the Goddess!"

The transition from earthly apotheosis to celestial triumph had happened so quickly and so smoothly that Mary felt no astonishment at being hailed as the object of this celebration. She looked radiant in her azure gown dazzling in the sunlight and set off by the scarlet ribbon of the Legion of Honor. Her entrance into paradise created more excitement than any angel or veteran archangel could recall. The enthusiasm aroused by the Son's ascension could not compare to the ardor glowing in these celestial hearts, for the Son came as a martyr mourned by a handful of sages—some called him a loser who never could bring himself to get back at his enemies. But Mary arrived in triumph. The strains of "Ave Maria" followed her into heaven and so enchanted the angels that they snatched up their trumpets to improvise an accompaniment.

Escorted thus by music-making hosts with pulsating wings, she came to the throne room where the Father sat, attended by the Holy Spirit and anxious courtiers.

"What's the meaning...?" the Father began sharply.

Mary silenced him with a gesture that made him shrivel on his throne. "Where is the Son?" she demanded in an imperious tone that nobody recalled having ever heard her use in paradise.

The Spirit alone seemed to retain his composure, explaining that the Son had deserted the palace long before and was occupying a neighboring throne.

"These family disputes are infantile and ridiculous," she announced in the same commanding voice. "Have someone go fetch me the Son!"

There was no need to find him. Caught by surprise along with everyone else and frantic to discover the source of all the excitement, the Son approached. He was still waited upon by a few loyal retainers, but most of them had yielded to the lure of the rising star and were beginning to dance attendance on her. Without further ado they joined the angels to celebrate the good tidings.

"Glory to our mother!" sang the heavenly choirs. "Glory to the queen of heaven! Beloved mother, Maria, Mater, Mutter, Meter, Demeter! You are our only Goddess! The Father, the Son, and the Spirit are mere demigods—really thirds of a god—and the proof is that the three of them had to get together to make the one, which is only an illusion anyway."

"Do you hear that, the three of you?" said Mary, addressing the Trinity. "I didn't put those words of wisdom in their mouths. Eternal truth emerges at last, after centuries of alienation and misrepresentation. You who have usurped the title of Father, are you prepared to surrender to me the throne you occupy in defiance of all justice?"

The Father leaped up in indignation, darting questioning glances at the circle of venerable archangels who remained loyal to him. Most of them wavered, but self-esteem ultimately prompted several not to deny him. They signaled their readiness to do combat in his name—formal combat, of course—for the rebellious hosts were muttering and snarling.

This final combat never took place. As the tiny band of the faithful prepared for slaughter, a fresh uproar announced the arrival of an archangel taller and more handsome than the noblest seraph. It was Michael, steadfast Michael, paragon of fealty and custodian of the palace. The ranks opened to let him pass. He approached the Goddess, fell to his knees, and, with a sweeping gesture denoting his vassalage, laid at her feet the flaming sword, symbol of his status and power. Behind him, the venerable praetorian-guard escort imitated his movement.

The crowd applauded. Beaming now, Mary told the archangel to rise.

The Father hung his head. "Thou too, Michael!" he murmured. Realizing the struggle was over, he resigned himself to defeat. "What's to become of me?" he ventured timidly.

Mary thought a moment and replied, "I authorize you and the Son to sit at my right and my left as a token of past services rendered."

"Will I be on the right or the left?" the Son inquired eagerly.

"Excuse me," the Father countered, "but I claim..."

They were off on another round of those tedious arguments about prerogatives that had been sowing trouble in paradise for centuries. The crowd began to mutter again. Mary called for silence and spoke sharply, an angry glint in her divine eyes. "Be quiet, you two!

If this is how you're going to behave, if you insist on infecting the heavens with your stupid quarrels, I've a mind to throw you out and never let you show your faces again in paradise."

"Do it, beloved mother! Do it, Goddess! You are omnipotent and we stand behind you!"

Confronted with these hostile demonstrations, which threatened to get worse, the Son finally yielded. "Forgive me, beloved mother, Goddess of the skies," he implored. "Your sovereign will shall be done. I'll sit wherever you say, only please let me stay next to you. I swear not to argue with the Father anymore."

"I do too, divine mother," the Father vowed, "and I bow to your supreme will. Don't send me away; I wouldn't know where to go. Satan has no use for me, and I couldn't bear the disgrace of exile. From now on I'll simply transmit your orders and see that they're carried out. I promise to make up with the Son."

"Unconditionally and forever?" Mary demanded severely.

"Unconditionally and forever," came a submissive duet from the pair.

Mary's tense features relaxed in a faint smile. "Then I agree," she said. "You'll both sit either on my right or my left, depending on what I decide, but in a respectful posture, like obedient sons. Embrace each other to mark this reconciliation, and peace be with you. Your sins will be forgiven."

The Father and the Son embraced each other and

· · · 187 · · ·

wept, then prostrated themselves as resounding cheers made the celestial clouds vibrate in celebration of the reconciliation and the promise of eternal peace in paradise. Mary seated herself majestically on the divine throne. The Father and Son crouched before her. Suddenly a scowl darkened her countenance. "I've forgotten to settle accounts with the Third Person," she declared. "Holy Spirit, manifest yourself if you are there and come forward to do me homage."

But the palace remained silent. The Holy Spirit gave no sign, and in the centuries to come Mary never heard a word from him. He had fled the skies and returned to earth, where, with his friend Marcole and a handful of other philosopher-scientists, he discovered in the search for undisclosed truth the peace and serenity he had never known before.

No divinity had the power to recall him to heaven, not even the new Goddess of the skies.

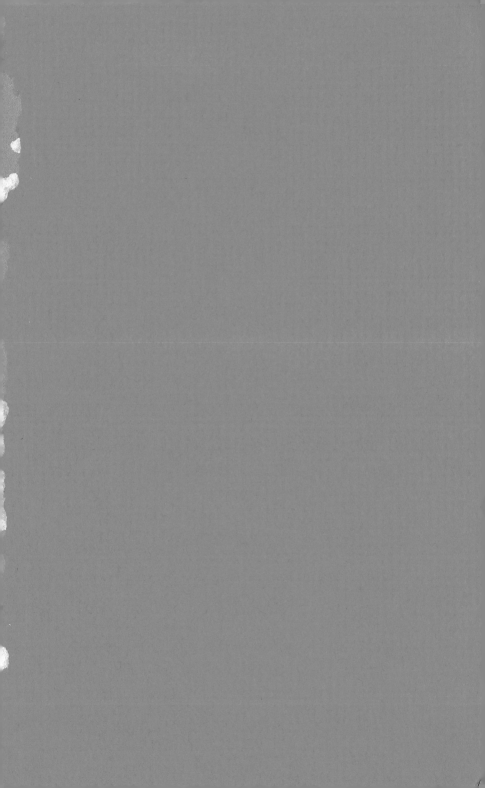